HOW TO HOLD A WOMAN

an imprint of Dzanc Books
3629 N. Hoyne
Chicago, IL 60618
www.ovbooks.org
othervoices@listserv.uic.edu

Published 2009 by Other Voices Books, an imprint of Dzanc Books
Book design by Steven Seighman
Cover photo by Robin Hann

09 10 11 5 4 3 2 1
First Edition June 2009

ISBN-13: 978-0-9767177-5-1
ISBN: 0976717751

Printed in the United States of America

HOW TO HOLD A WOMAN

a novel in stories

Billy Lombardo

For Nina and Donna Jean

CHAPTER 1

At Khyber Pass
(August 2002)

Curbside at the United terminal, Alan Taylor looks for a green Mazda with his wife in the driver's seat, three kids in the back. He supposes Audrey will have shoulder-length brown hair but it has been two months and she has surprised him before. After the Africa trip—Izzy was still a baby then—Audrey had picked him up from the airport, her hair clipped like a boy's in summer.

He wonders what she'll be wearing—something white, he thinks—how she will kiss him in the car. The cops will be hurrying cars through the terminal, blowing whistles and waving arms, but still. So much in that first kiss home.

When the Mazda pulls to the curb, Isabel springs from the backseat to hug him. She is wearing blue shorts and a yellow tank top. Alan is surprised at the fullness of her hug. At her back Alan feels the strap and clasp of a bra. Twelve years old, Isabel. From a girl to a woman. Two months he has been gone. Jesus.

Alan waves to Audrey while something in Isabel's hand edges into his back. Audrey smiles and waves. A whistle blows.

In the car Sammy says, "Hey, Dad, my ears popped when you slammed the trunk." Sammy unbuckles his car seat to kiss his father. Alan watches while Sammy buckles himself back in.

Audrey says hi and kisses Alan on the lips, her fingers on his cheek. Her lips are full and soft as she kisses him. Her fingers trace his cheek above the line of his jaw.

It is dark and damp in the shadow of the terminal but from Audrey's kiss Alan knows what the weather was like in Chicago that afternoon, knows that Audrey showered in the morning and spent the afternoon in the sun. Swiveling in the love seat on the patio, reading in the sun.

Another whistle from the cop outside.

"All right, all right, already," Audrey says. She is looking into Alan's eyes still.

"Khyber Pass?" Isabel says.

"Khyber Pass," Audrey says.

It is Alan's favorite restaurant, Khyber Pass. The welcome home restaurant.

Audrey checks her mirrors, glances over her shoulder, and pulls carefully into the terminal traffic. She is wearing her yellow sundress with orange flowers—tiger lilies—that seem to be spilling from it. When she is comfortably in her new lane she looks at Alan again.

"I thought you might have grown a beard," she says. "I shaved at the airport," Alan says. "I thought I might be kissing you tonight."

Audrey smiles.

"Where's Dex?" Alan says.

"Baseball practice," Audrey says. "Team sleepover tonight at one of the kids' houses."

"All-stars," Sammy says. "The eight-year-olds have all-stars and sleepovers."

Audrey checks the rearview mirror, then the side mirror, and merges into another lane.

"Are we okay, Mommy?" Sammy says.

Audrey stretches to see him in the rearview mirror.

"We're fine," she says.

"So," Isabel begins.

"Dad?" Sammy says. "When will I get to play baseball?"

"When you're five," Alan says, and Sammy opens his hand and spreads his fingers. He watches the back of his hand while his thumb appears and disappears, appears again.

"Next summer, sweetie," Audrey says. She leans toward Alan. "Every day I get this," she whispers. "He asks me every day."

In the fleeting silence that follows, Isabel speaks again.

"So," she begins.

"Some of the kids on Dex's team are terrible," Sammy says. "Aren't they, Mommy?"

"They're trying their best," Audrey says.

"Mitch is terrible," Sammy says.

Audrey looks at Alan and nods apologetically, lips the word *terrible*, stretches it and wears it like a mask on her face.

"Sammy has become best friends with a boy named Tegan," Isabel says.

Alan can feel Isabel growing in the backseat, setting her brother's interest above her own. Like a mother. Altruism belongs to humans alone, he thinks. There are no such gestures among juvenile ring-tailed lemurs in Madagascar. No such gestures anywhere in Kingdom Animalia.

"Tegan is an Aries," Audrey says.

"All of Sammy's friends are fire signs," Isabel says.

Audrey looks at her watch. "They haven't seen each other since one o'clock, Tegan and Sammy. It's the longest they've been apart all summer."

Audrey checks her mirrors again.

"Are we okay?" Sammy says.

"We're fine, sweetie," Audrey says, stretching again to see him in the mirror. "I promise you we're not lost, Sammy."

Isabel asks Alan about his research trip. He glances at Audrey, does not say it was great. He leans over the seat and turns toward Sammy but looks at Isabel first so that she knows this answer belongs to her as well.

"Madagascar has a tree you would love, Sammy," he says. "In all, they have nearly two hundred species of palms, the most famous of which is the fan-shaped Ravinala palm. *Ravenala madagascariensis*. They call it the traveler's tree," he says. "It follows the sun's movement from east to west, and so if you ever get lost you can figure out where to go by looking at the tree."

There is no air-conditioning in the Mazda, and so the windows are rolled down. The radio is on but no one seems to be listening. Alan wonders how many new songs are written in a summer. If he could hear them over the wind swirling through the windows from River Road, would he know the words? They listen to the wind. They listen to Sammy who complains of being four years old in a world where eight-year-olds are the luckiest things and how lucky it must be to be eight and still playing baseball in August. They listen to Isabel who begins several times to speak but never gets past "So" without Sammy returning to baseball. Over Alan's shoulder, Isabel rolls her eyes at her brother's interruptions, and Alan nods. They will have time to catch up later. Alan touches Audrey's yellow, tiger-lilied leg. Audrey smiles and in her hand on his is the summer he missed.

Alan walks from the car to the restaurant carrying Sammy and holding Isabel's hand. Sammy turns the hold into a squeezing hug during the half-block walk to Khyber Pass. It makes Alan laugh, and so Sammy does it again, does it several times as they walk. Alan laughs every time. By the time they reach the restaurant Isabel is laughing. Her hand is like a woman's hand in her father's grip.

They are the first customers for dinner at Khyber Pass. Audrey is not even certain the restaurant is open; she shades her eyes with her hand and looks in without trying the door and a waiter waves them inside. Stringed music is playing. An instrument with hundreds of strings, it seems to Alan.

Audrey enters one side of the booth they are directed toward and Alan follows. Across from them, Sammy enters first, then Isabel. Alan takes his first good look at them. How sun-darkened they are! In the soft yellow light of Khyber Pass they are brown children. Sammy reaches for a juice glass filled with crayons against the mirrored wall of the booth. He takes a black crayon from the glass and begins to draw on the butcher paper that covers the tablecloth, the scroll of the paper springing above Alan's thigh.

On the table in front of Isabel is a hardcover copy of The Great Gatsby. At the airport, when Isabel hugged him at the curb, he had felt something poke against his back. This book.

"Isabel spent the entire summer at the pool," Audrey says. "Mornings at dance lessons, afternoons at the pool."

It seems to Alan as though Audrey was seeing the children—Isabel now—with his eyes.

"She's been babysitting two nights a week for Sandy and Ed across the street," Audrey says. "And just tonight, on our way to the airport, she finished her summer reading for humanities."

Audrey leans slightly into Alan's shoulder. Like a girlfriend.

"She has fallen in love with Daisy Buchanan," Audrey says of Isabel.

Across the booth, Isabel nods, smiles her coy confession.

"And our dance performance this summer was a Jazz Age theme," Isabel says. "We have a DVD of the performance at home," Audrey says.

"May I share something with you in this book, Dad?" Isabel says.

Alan looks at Audrey at this way of speaking of Isabel's, which seems new to him, and Audrey smiles. It's true, she seems to say. This is Isabel.

"You may," Alan says.

Sammy is bent over his drawing, his tongue in the easy bite of his teeth.

"When did you last read The Great Gatsby?" Isabel says.

"It's been years," Alan says.

"Well, of course you remember Gatsby," Isabel says.

"Of course."

"Certainly," Isabel says. "And Daisy?"

"Of course," Alan says.

"Well, at one of Gatsby's parties," Isabel says, "Daisy says this to Nick Carraway, the narrator. I memorized it."

For a moment, Isabel settles into a preparatory silence, closes her eyes and shifts, it seems, within her skin. It is as though something is taking place beneath the brown skin of her. Isabel becomes someone else in the booth at Khyber Pass. Daisy Buchanan's words spring from her as though they have been bubbling in her throat for days, and in her eyes it seems that Alan has become Nick Carraway.

"If you want to kiss me any time during the evening, Nick, just let me know and I'll be glad to arrange it for you. Just mention my name."

Alan smiles, glances at Audrey, at this child they have grown, and claps softly. Isabel shrugs her tank-topped shoulders.

"Nick Carraway is Daisy's cousin, but I don't care," Isabel says. "I think it's sweet, anyway."

Sammy pulls a blue crayon from the small glass against the wall and begins to color again.

Isabel shifts in her seat. "May I tell you another thing that Daisy says?"

"Certainly," Alan says, smiling at Audrey.

At Khyber Pass Isabel slides from the booth and stands at the table as slenderly as Daisy Buchanan, and as she introduces the scene she adds something to her boyish hips, begins to sway.

"Before that kiss me scene," Isabel says—she sways still, through the narration she sways; Alan knows she has rehearsed these words, this sway, in her bedroom, her door closed and locked against the world. Her hiplessness seems to disappear as Alan considers looking at Audrey again, but does not.

"Nick is telling Daisy of his recent visit to Chicago," Isabel begins, "and in this scene, Daisy responds to Nick's Chicago visit."

Isabel touches the tips of her fingers to her cheek and tilts her head, but snaps out of character for one final narrative setup.

"Oh," she says, "I should remind you that Tom Buchanan is Daisy's husband."

Isabel sways, snaps again.

"He's a jerk," she says. "Here we go."

She sways like Daisy.

"Do they miss me?" she says in Daisy's voice.

She shifts without moving her feet, and Isabel is Nick Carraway. Youthful and charming.

13

"The whole town is desolate," Isabel's Carraway says. All the cars have the left rear wheel painted black as a mourning wreath and there's a persistent wail all night along the North Shore."

Isabel shifts again—without moving, it seems—and she is Daisy once more.

"How gorgeous! Let's go back, Tom. Tomorrow!"

Alan and Audrey clap gently and glance at each other. Isabel bows and returns to the booth.

The waiter steps carefully toward the booth holding four glasses of water. Alan distributes the glasses as the waiter walks away.

"Bravo," he says to Isabel.

Isabel turns then to look at Sammy, still coloring on the butcher paper.

"Would you like to hear another reason why they call the Ravinala palm the traveler's tree?" Alan says.

"Certainly," Isabel says.

"At the base of the leaf stalks of the Ravenala madagascariensis," Alan begins, "there is contained a supply of pure water to aid thirsty travelers." He takes a green crayon and on the paper in front of him he begins to draw a leaf of the Ravinala palm.

Across the table Sammy lengthens briefly in his seat to look at what his father is drawing.

"What is it called?" he says.

"Ravenala madagascariensis," Alan says.

"No," Sammy says. "The other name."

"The traveler's tree," Alan says.

Sammy lowers his head to his artwork and speaks again.

"We got lost at the ethnic festival in Evanston," he says. "Me and Izzy and Dex," and Alan stops drawing. "While you were gone," Sammy says.

Isabel nods. "It was my fault," she says. "For an hour we were lost."

Sammy looks up at Isabel as she speaks.

"Mom was getting us egg rolls and she told us to wait near the drinking fountain, but a train of dancers with bells and scarves like gypsies came past."

Audrey wipes at the paper tablecloth as though to brush its crumbs on her lap.

"People in the audience began to follow the gypsy dancers," Isabel says. "There was a long line of people behind them."

Sammy, with his violet crayon, is drawing a boy horizontal to the ground, catching a line drive on a baseball diamond.

"Dex told Isabel that we should stay by the fountain," Sammy says.

"I've already said it was my fault, Sammy," Isabel says.

"We're all here now, and we're fine," Audrey says, but Isabel seems to be caught between the story and an apology.

"I thought I knew the way back," she says. "But the long line of dancers and regular people held hands and circled the stage a couple of times and when the dance ended it was like we were in a different place."

"Can we talk about something else?" Sammy says.

"Nothing was familiar," Isabel says. "I couldn't find the fountain."

Audrey is still brushing crumbs onto her lap.

"When I returned to the fountain with the egg rolls I panicked," Audrey says. "I ran through the park calling their names. There were children everywhere. I thought I saw them dozens of times. I hadn't noticed how many children there were. It seemed as though I was looking into the faces of thousands of children as I ran through the grounds.

"I keep having dreams that they're lost," Audrey says, wiping crumbs still. "Three since it happened in June." Alan puts his hand on her tiger lilies.

"In my dreams," she says, "when I think I find them, their faces turn into strangers."

Audrey sips from her glass of water, wipes its sweat with her cloth napkin.

"I must have looked crazed," she says. "And then I looked up and there they were, standing next to a policeman at the edge of the stage."

"Do we have to talk about this?" Sammy says. The heels of Isabel's hands are at the edge of the table and she raises her fingers to ask her mother to end the story, and the story ends.

The food arrives. Lamb and chicken and vegetarian couscous, pita bread, rice, dipping sauces. Sammy and Isabel fix plates for themselves. Sammy forks his food into compartments so their edges do not touch. Isabel smiles at her triangles of pita.

While Isabel spoons couscous onto her plate she shapes her lips into kisses, shapes the word *couscous* under her breath.

"Couscous."

Repeats it.

"Couscous," she says. "Couscous."

Sammy joins her.

Audrey joins her.

And at Khyber Pass, while they prepare their plates—while Sammy and Audrey join Isabel in a couscous chorus—Alan recalls an afternoon he had spent in Madagascar that summer. He had been observing his lemurs all morning when five juvenile savanna baboons drew into the area and frightened the family of lemurs away. The baboons discovered a fallen baobab tree some thirty yards to Alan's left. A free limb of the old tree jutted out like a diving board and one of the male baboons scaled the limb. He seemed to test the bouncing play of the tree while he scaled it, climbed up it and worked with its spring, descended and climbed again, and looked over the edge of the tree into a pool of water—a temporary gift of the rainy season—as though he were a child considering his first dive. On his final ascent, then, the baboon leaped onto the farthest extension of the tree and bounced into the pool of water. The rest of the baboons followed the leader, and for three hours they scaled the tree, bounced on the limb, and flung themselves into the pool. A hundred times or more they scaled the tree, they bounced, they splashed in the ephemeral pool.

And at Khyber Pass, while Audrey begins to eat, while Sammy sees to the compartmentalization of his food, while Isabel falls in love with the word couscous, while Dex takes infield practice for rookie baseball, Alan begins to cry. It is tearless, mostly. A small wetness at the edge of his eyes, like the tears of a yawn. If he were alone, he thinks, he could let loose. Weep. He could allow convulsive sobs to shake his shoulders and rattle the table, clink silverware against plates, tinkle ice cubes against glasses until he pulled his elbows back from the table to spill an infinity of tears into the cup of his hands. But he catches it in time, he thinks. He pinches softly the bridge of his nose and tells himself, I am back now. I have returned.

Neither Audrey nor Sammy nor Isabel speaks.

Sammy looks up, at the change in the silence, Alan thinks, and then he draws a White Sox baseball cap flying from the head of his crayoned baseball player.

Audrey says nothing, but she switches her fork to her left hand and sets her right hand on Alan's knee. Isabel smiles a closed-lip smile and tilts her head as though Alan has given her something. A flower.

At Khyber Pass, when his unspent tears finally feather into fluttering breaths, Alan wipes his eyes with his cloth napkin and spreads it on his lap.

"You okay, Dad?" Isabel says.

"Yeah," Alan says, "I'm okay."

He wipes a triangle of bread across the hummus plate.

"I just missed you guys," he says. "And I wish I could have been at the festival."

It is quiet for a moment. Until Sammy says, "Couscous," and looks up as though he has made a joke.

Isabel musses Sammy's hair then, and says couscous, too.

"Couscous," she says, and she looks up at her father and winks.

"Couscous," Alan says.

"Couscous," Audrey says.

Isabel brushes away pita crumbs, which had fallen on her book, and without looking up she speaks again.

"Dad?" she says.

"Yes?" Alan says, and Isabel brushes her hand across the book again.

"If you want to kiss me any time during the evening," she says, "just let me know."

CHAPTER 2

How I Knew You Were Mad at Me
(June 2004)

1. You broke your promise to make potato pancakes.

It seemed to begin on Father's Day. Way back when, you had promised me you would make my favorite breakfast every Father's Day until the end of time, and I also knew you were planning on it because there was a produce bag filled with red potatoes in the pantry. The kicker, though, was that there was sour cream in the refrigerator, and there was never sour cream in the house unless you were going to make potato pancakes, because for some reason the thought of sour cream—the color and the texture—makes you sick, and this was supposed to be some kind of proof to me of something, that you allowed sour cream in the house for me on Father's Day. Like it was some kind of a gift. Like, *This is how much I love you* or something. But you never made them.

2. You salted and peppered the hash browns that I was making.

And so I ended up making the same old Sunday breakfast as always: either French toast or waffles or pancakes with hash browns and bacon; this time it was French toast. And while the bacon was cooking on the front left burner and the hash browns were cooking on the front right burner, I set the dining room table and then went into the boys' room to see if they were up yet, which is when I started thinking you were mad because of how late I let them stay up, and when I came back into the kitchen you were salting and peppering the hash browns that I was making. And the thing is, I would never think of coming into the kitchen and adding garlic to your tomato sauce, or when you make meatballs I would never sneak an egg in the meat even though your meatballs are kind of dry, but there you were salting and peppering the hash browns that *I* was making, and you know how much I hate that. Like I was going to forget to do it. Or like I was always getting the amount of them wrong.

3. You brought your own napkin and fork for breakfast but I had already set the table.

So I doubled a paper bag and put the bacon in it and shook it gently, and even you agree that this is the best way to deal with bacon when it is fried, and when the burner was freed up I put the double griddle for the French toast on the left side of the stove top. Meanwhile, you were slamming the pedal of the toaster down and just waiting there for it to toast with your arms pressed across your chest, and then I dipped the French toast in the batter and laid it out on the griddle and then started rotating the French toast around like a Rubik's Cube so it would cook evenly, and when it was just about ready I got a dinner plate from the cupboard and piled the French toast on it. I walked into the dining room to set the French toast on the table and when I turned around I almost bumped into you. You were right there with the bowl of hash browns and the double-bagged bacon on the little black plate, and the toast that you made by slamming and slamming the pedal of the toaster, and you also had another napkin and another fork inside another glass in your hand, as though I had forgotten to put a setting out for someone else. And you looked at the table and saw there were already four settings of everything, and then you looked at me like *I* was crazy. And then you slammed down all of the stuff on the table. You picked up a glass and plate and fork and napkin that I had already set there, and you glared at me, and you didn't say anything. You just took the things I had set down and slammed them back in the cabinets and drawers where they belonged. But I didn't say anything. It was obvious that you were mad.

4. When the boys finally woke up you didn't even look at them.

When the food was on the table, I went to get the boys again and finally they were awake, but I ended up wrestling with them for a minute until I heard you open the front door and check for the mail even though it was Sunday. I thought for a minute that you were going to slam the door even though you used to say you would never slam the door. Your mother was a door slammer, you used to say—a pincher and a door slammer and a shut upper—and you never wanted to be any of those. So you didn't slam the door. You shut the door of the mailbox pretty hard, though, and I knew that meant that you wanted us to eat now and so I walked into the dining room. Sammy was on my shoulders and Dex was holding on to the back of my belt and making me slide him across the floor. Come on, Dad, Dex was saying, let me get on your shoulders, and I was like, Dex, you're like twenty years old, and he was like, I'm only ten, and Sammy was like, You have to be six, though, Dex, you have to be six to still go on Dad's shoulders, and I could feel Sammy laughing and swiveling his head back to look at Dex sliding across the floor.

And when we got to the dining room you had just turned the corner from the kitchen and that was it. You didn't even say good morning to them. It was clear to everyone that you were not in the mood for laughing, but they had the giggles and so I gave them the look and we started eating in the silence that you seemed so intent on.

I sprinkled powdered sugar on my French toast and then poured syrup around it like a moat around a castle. Dex and Sammy started to laugh at the sound of the syrup when I squeezed it from the plastic bottle, but I didn't laugh. I asked Sammy to get the cranberry juice from the refrigerator and he immediately got up so that he could laugh in the kitchen where you wouldn't see him, and Dex shot up from his chair and said he was going to get the orange juice, and I wished there was one other thing we needed from the kitchen but there wasn't, so I just sat there in the gray room with you. When the boys came back into the dining room it was like they were walking into a sea of gloom.

5. Hash browns and toast were all that you ate for breakfast.

The boys started eating as fast as they could. I didn't tell them to slow down. I knew they wanted to get out from under your darkness. The only sounds were the squeaks of our forks on our plates, the crunch of bacon, and the sound of swallowing. You spooned some hash browns onto a piece of toast and folded the bread over it and started to eat it like a half sandwich. It would have been fine if it just seemed to us that you didn't want to be there, but it was like *we* were not even there. It was as if that's what you wanted: for *us* not to be there. And so, just to be ornery, I asked weren't you going to have any French toast, and you said no, and I knew that's what you were doing, only eating the stuff that you were in on, and the thing is, you didn't even make the hash browns. I did. So maybe you should have only had toast, if you were so mad at me.

6. After breakfast you started cleaning loudly.

Always the vacuum cleaner banging into the legs of things, and also you vacuum the hardwood floors so that I can hear it even when I'm downstairs studying or during the school year when I'm grading papers or tests or while I'm in the room with the boys watching television, the cabinets slamming and the pots clanging against each other from their hooks in the pantry. The dishes banging with your madness.

7. *You* drove the car to Home Depot.

You insisted that we both go to look at ceiling fans, and so I called my sister and asked her if she could come over to stay with the boys while we went to Home Depot for a little while. While we waited for her, all you did was sigh heavily and look at the clock and then look at me like it was my sister's fault that we didn't have a decent ceiling fan. When the doorbell rang, you said, *Finally*, and I knew that's exactly what Dex and Sammy were thinking, too. I could hear them laughing with my sister as soon as she walked upstairs to see them.

You took the keys from the dish on the hallway table and waited for me while I looked for my green jacket, which I just gave up trying to find after a while. And then you started huffing while I tied my shoes like I was the one thing that had been holding you up for six years to get the fucking ceiling fan. And when I finally had my shoes tied you were standing with your back against the door and you hardly left me enough room to pass through. You couldn't just walk outside to give me a little berth, though. And I'm sure the only reason you didn't slam the door is because my sister was there and she would have heard it. Then you locked the door and when I put my hand out for the keys so I could drive like I always do, you said, *I'll drive.*

8. You walked in the rain as though it wasn't even raining.

There was a light rain outside, but in the house it wasn't raining at all, and probably it wouldn't have seemed too bad if I had found my jacket, but I didn't, and so it seemed to me like it was a lot of rain falling. And so when I walked around to the passenger side of the car, I lifted my shoulders and squinted against the rain like an elderly person until I saw you walking to the driver's side like you were Steve McQueen, and then I pretended it didn't bother me either, but it was too late.

9. While we drove to Home Depot in the rain you waited a long time to put the wipers on.

It was raining pretty lightly, but still, you could have set the wipers on one of the intermittent levels, it's not like that would have killed you. It's not like that would have made me think you weren't mad anymore. By the time we got to the

end of the alley, the tiny dots of rain were beginning to fill
the windshield pretty totally and I was going to say something
when we got to Madison Street, but I knew what you were
doing and I wasn't going to let you know that it was getting
hard to see. I was thinking pretty soon it's going to get
hard for you to see, too, and then you'll put the wipers on.
And then at Jackson I looked over at you like, *Okay, I get
it, Audrey. I know you're mad. But try to remember it's not
just you and me, okay? We still have two boys at home. Now
could you just put the wipers on, it's getting hard to see.* But
I didn't say anything. I just looked at you. You didn't turn
them on until we got to Roosevelt, and I thought maybe
you would keep them on, but you didn't keep them on. You
waited again until we turned on Cermak, or Twenty-sixth
Street, I get them mixed up, and that was it until we got to
Home Depot.

10. After three days of silence, you slammed the bathroom door.

Then it was the silent treatment, which you've become
amazing at. For the next three days you didn't come near
any of us. You didn't say good morning or good night to me,
and you didn't go into the boys' room and say good night
to them, either. You didn't go to the store or make dinner
or anything. We would go out whenever we could because
that's what it seemed like you wanted us to do. We would
go to the park to take fielding practice or go to the batting
cages or to get beef sandwiches at Johnny's and when we
came home you would be gone. You wouldn't leave a note or
anything, and you would be gone for hours.

Then this morning we Rollerbladed to the park to
play tennis, and while Dex and Sammy took off their skates
on the porch I came into the house and started to look

around to see if you were home and when I just about got to the bedroom I heard the bathroom door slam, but you slammed it so hard that the thing didn't catch and the door popped open some. Through the sliver of the open door I saw you. Your top was off. You were sitting on the closed seat of the toilet in just your underwear. There were criss-crossed scratches of new blood across your breasts and you were crying. Your head was back and your throat looked like it belonged to someone else, the way it was exposed, and your breasts were bleeding and your eyes were closed and raised to the ceiling and you were crying. Your fingers were raised in helpless claws on your bare legs.

I didn't hear Dex and Sammy come in the house. They had grown used to the silence, had begun to move in a silence of their own. When I looked up they were right next to me. I shut the door so they wouldn't see you, but it may have been too late.

It may have been too late.

The door wasn't even closed.

You slammed the door so hard you thought it was shut, but it wasn't.

That's how mad you were.

CHAPTER 3

The Business of Night
(September 2006)

Audrey put her toothbrush in a travel tube and tapped it against her palm as she walked to her closet, still smiling from the surprise she'd saved for the boys: dinner and an overnight at their father's apartment. They were on the sidewalk outside of school when she told them. Dex, who was in sixth grade, had shouted, *Yes!* and pumped his arm like an athlete. Sammy, who was in third grade, set his bag on the sidewalk and danced.

"Please don't dance," Dex had said. "Not here, Sammy."

Audrey pulled the light string and leaned against the doorjamb, angling her head in the deep left of the closet. She pushed aside thicknesses of clothes—blouses, pants, dresses—until she found the white nightgown. She brushed the back of her hand against it. June, July, August. It had been three months and a few days since Alan had left. Longer still since she'd worn the nightgown. She tilted the padded hanger to one side and then the other, and as the gown floated onto the bend of her arm the tiny hairs at her wrist trembled at attention.

She had never intended to buy it. On the April day that she walked into Charlotte's she had tried it on because she was on spring break from Francis Parker where she taught English. She had tried it on because Sammy was at Tegan's house and Dex was at Jack Murphy's. She had tried it on because it was sunny outside and because there was time before she had to pick up the boys from baseball practice. Also, the moon was in Leo. She stood with her back to the mirror as she slipped the nightgown over her head and smoothed it over her body. She turned around quickly to surprise herself in the mirror, and in the lamplight of the dressing room, the black divan behind her, she could not remember ever looking better. Not in the last two years, at least. The nightgown fit like skin everywhere—at her breasts and waist and across her bottom—and it fluttered like a veil at the top of her thighs. It was a nightdress, really—lacy and soft—and it was charged with something. Audrey felt like a woman again, like her girl-hood imaginings of what a woman should be, and she smiled at her reflection. An actual smile. She thought of kissing the mirror but twirled before it instead. And then she reclined on the divan like something worshipped.

She did not wear it for Alan that same day. Whatever she had felt in the boutique that afternoon was gone by the time she returned home. In fact, she was not sure she had even spoken to Alan that night. But on a Saturday soon after, the sun had come out and it was in the low seventies all day and Audrey had soaked in the warmth and the light in a sun-dress all afternoon, and when the boys had gone to bed, she put the nightdress on for Alan.

It was May. They were still together then. She had tiptoed into the bathroom while Alan washed his face at the sink. She waited until he saw her reflection in the mirror and then he turned around.

"What's going on?" he said.

"Nothing," Audrey said, and she stood there quietly while Alan eyed her nightdress.

"That's a nice little number," he said.

"I miss you," she said.

There was only the sound of the faucet running behind him.

"You got some sun today, too," he said, and she nodded.

"I miss you, Alan," she said again.

Alan looked in her eyes.

"I've been here all along," he said, and Audrey nodded.

When Alan turned back to the sink to dry his face, Audrey thought about returning the nightdress. She thought about turning around and going to bed, but she didn't. She walked up to Alan and hugged him from behind. She slipped her hands in his boxers and brushed her fingernails along his legs. She rested her chin on his shoulder and told him she was sorry. Then she pulled downward at the hem of his boxers, but as his weight was pressed against the sink, his boxers didn't slip off easily. After a second tugging she pulled them down and left them in a puddle at his feet. Alan edged away from the cold of the sink then, and Audrey had room to touch him. She reached around him to turn off the faucet first.

Alan lingered there holding the washcloth. In the mirror, Audrey saw that his eyes were closed. When he finally turned around to face her, Audrey raised herself to her toes and lifted the billowy hem of the beautiful nightdress—under which she wore nothing—and offered herself to him.

May, that was. Just before they separated. And against her skin the nightdress seemed the whitest thing.

She would wear it again tonight.

The boys seemed to find nothing peculiar in the plans for the night. What about it was peculiar? Alan and

Audrey were still married, weren't they? Isn't this what struggling married couples did, how they muddled through? Split up sometimes and had overnights sometimes to give the kids some semblance of family? Didn't it even serve as a model to children of how parents worked at things?

In the hallway, Dex's backpack leaned against the front door. Audrey started to open the main section, but the cloth of the pack stretched over the squared edges of what she knew must be the Monopoly box inside. She would be tempted to reorganize everything within if it exploded open as it threatened to do at the zipper's next advance, so she let it be. She folded the nightgown and leaned over to stuff it, along with her toothbrush, in the mesh pocket on the side of the bag next to a deck of cards. She packed her reading glasses in the pocket as well, and when she looked up Dex was waiting. He held a football in one hand and pounded it against the other.

"Ready?" he said.

"Ready," Audrey said. Dex was eleven and it was hard not to see Alan in him. Skin, eyes, hair. As dark as his father. Audrey chewed on the inside of her mouth.

"What's wrong?" Dex said.

"Nothing. Why?"

"You're biting your cheek."

"I'm fine," she said. "Where's Sammy?"

"On the phone. Dad said to wait for him outside the Treasure Island. He's picking up stuff for dinner."

"Did you pack your toothbrush?" Audrey asked.

"Yes."

"Pajamas?"

"Yes, Mom."

Audrey lifted the backpack with a mock grunt.

"Yikes," she said. "What's in this thing?"

"You said to pack everything in one bag," Dex said.

"My intention was to keep you from overpacking," Audrey said. She looped her arms into the straps and loosened them—half hopping to settle its weight against her back. Sammy turned the corner into the hallway. Against the gray of his gray sweatshirt, his eyes—hazel in the light of day—looked gray.

"Dad said to meet him—"

"I told her already," Dex said.

"Dad said to meet him at the Treasure Island," Sammy said.

"I told her, Sammy."

"Did you tell her what Dad's making for dinner?"

Dex glared at Sammy.

"Go ahead, Dex. Why don't you tell Mom what Dad's making for dinner?" Sammy crossed his arms and shifted his weight to one hip.

"You need to respect your elders," Dex said.

"That's what I thought," Sammy said. He looked at his mother again. "Dad has dough rising for personal pizzas."

"Excellent," she said.

"Let's go," Dex said, and they walked down the carpeted stairs of the darkened hallway and into the world.

Wells Street was the color of shadow, but at Goethe, at Schiller, at North—where the sun was a fiery ball in the lowest inches of the sky—the streets were orange. Across from Treasure Island Foods they stopped to wait for Alan. Dex lifted the backpack from his mother's shoulders.

"Off with the bag," he said. "You're the ref, and it might get ugly."

Audrey slipped her arms from the straps and Dex set the backpack against the iron fence of the Wells Street Apartments.

"Pass only, no rush," Dex said.

"One down each?" Sammy asked.

"Yeah. All or nothing," Dex said. "If you don't score a touchdown on one play, it's a turnover. Your ball, Sammy."

Audrey leaned on a parking meter and looked over her shoulder at the doors to the Treasure Island.

"Close your eyes," Sammy said, and while Dex closed his eyes, Sammy hiked the ball to himself. Dex counted out two seconds and turned around in place twice while Sammy picked an opportunity to run past him without capture. The next play was Dex's turn and Sammy's followed. Each play, it seemed, turned into a touchdown. As Audrey watched from her parking meter, her chin resting on the back of her hands, it seemed they were doing all right without a referee. She had never seen this game played before.

Audrey kept an eye on the door to Treasure Island while the boys ran patterns around parking meters. Passersby flinched and stutter-stepped in their wake. A homeless man with crossed and bloodshot eyes walked past them.

While Dex was scoring his sixth touchdown, Audrey looked across the street and saw Alan coming through the doors of the Treasure Island.

"Let's go, guys," she said.

Alan was wearing new pants. Pleated. Thick-ribbed corduroys, dark brown. His BlackBerry was attached to his belt. In three short years he had moved from an obsession with animal behavior to an obsession of law, had passed the bar exam and now was working as an attorney for the Chicago Police. He wore a BlackBerry now. Emails came from Alan's BlackBerry. Three years it had taken to become someone else.

"Hike," Sammy said.

"This one doesn't count," Dex said. "I'm not even there."

"Game off," Audrey called again. "Your father's here."

"Damn," Dex said.

Audrey turned around toward Dex's voice. "What did you say?"

"The backpack," Dex said.

Audrey kept her eyes on Dex. "Did you say *damn?*"

"Someone took the backpack, Mom," Dex said.

Audrey looked at the fence where the bag had been, and then back at Alan in the middle of the street. He wore a new jacket as well. Black. The groceries were in two paper bags in his arms as he stepped onto the sidewalk.

"What's going on?" he said.

"Sammy's backpack is gone," Dex said.

"What happened?" Alan asked.

"Someone took it," Sammy said.

"It's my fault," Dex said. "I should've left it on Mom's back. It would've still been there."

"It's okay, Dex," Alan said. "How long have you been here?"

"Five minutes," Audrey said. "Hi."

"More like ten," Dex said.

Alan smiled at Audrey, his lips closed. He set the bags next to the iron fence where the backpack had been.

"It's my fault," Dex said.

"It's not your fault." Alan said. He looked north and south on Wells Street. "Where was it last?"

"It was right there." Sammy pointed at the groceries. "Can you arrest someone?"

"I'm not a cop," Alan said. "I told you that." He kissed Sammy on the side of his face.

"Did you see anyone walk past?"

"Not really," Dex said.

"We were playing football," Sammy said.

"Dozens of people passed," Audrey said. She had planned to say something about Alan's pants and his new jacket. "The guy who sells *StreetWise* in front of Walgreen's, people coming from work, Starbucks. Dozens of people."

She had not intended for there to be a tone to her words, but Alan looked up at her as though there was definitely a tone.

Alan starting walking toward North Avenue but stopped when Audrey touched his arm above the elbow.

"Where are you going?" she said.

"To look around."

"And what'll you do if you find him?"

"It was a man?" Alan said.

Her hand was on Alan's arm still.

"You said *him*," Alan said. "It was a man who took it?"

"Of course it was a man," she said. "Women don't steal children's backpacks."

"You'd be surprised," Alan said.

"He's gone, Alan," she said. "Anyway, if he walked that way with it we would have seen him."

"If the backpack was right there, Audrey, you should've seen him anyway."

"Please don't fight," Sammy said.

"We're not fighting," Audrey said. She took her hand from Alan's arm. "He's gone," she said. "Just let it go."

Dex sat with his back against the iron fence. "It's my fault," he said again. He held his fingers at his temples, his voice broke. Audrey bent toward him.

"Sweetie, it's not your fault."

Dex looked up at his mother. Droplets held in his eyes.

"I think Smokey might've been in the backpack," he said.

"Oh, Dex."

Audrey sat next to him and put her hand on his knee.

"What do you mean you *think* it might've been in the backpack?" Alan asked.

Dex lifted his head toward his father, his lip trembling.

"I can't remember if I packed him or not. I think I might've packed him."

Sammy stood next to Alan and put his hand in his father's. "I don't think you packed it, Dex," he said. "I didn't see it when I put the Monopoly game in."

"I put more stuff in after that," Dex said. "And anyway, if we were packing for the night, why wouldn't I bring Smokey?"

Alan took Sammy's hand from his own. He pinched his pants above the knees and crouched toward Dex.

"Think back, Dex. Try to picture Smokey in your hand."

"I can't remember."

"Don't you think you would have remembered if you put him in the bag?"

"I don't know, Dad. I can't be sure."

Alan's BlackBerry buzzed. He pressed a button and the screen lit up.

Sammy peeked over Alan's shoulder at the screen. "Does that mean someone in the city just got killed, Dad?"

"Maybe so, Sammy," Alan said. He looked at Dex. "I'll tell you what, Dex. Why don't you and Sammy walk with your mother to the apartment, and I'll take a look around the block for the bag. Maybe they just took it and emptied it in the alley. What else was in it?"

"My pajamas and toothbrush," said Sammy. "And clothes for tomorrow."

Alan looked at Dex.

"Same," Dex said. "Our Game Boys were in it, too."

"Oh, yeah. That's right," Sammy said. He looked at Dex and sat next to him. He put his arm across his brother's shoulder. "It's all right, Dex. Dad'll find it."

Dex's lips shut tightly as Audrey pulled him closer.

Alan stood and caught Audrey's eye. "Were your things in the bag, too?"

"Glasses and toothbrush," she said.

"That's all you brought?"

"And something to sleep in."

Alan took his keys from his pocket and nodded toward the Treasure Island.

"Do you need anything?"

What she needed—what Audrey wanted—was ten minutes of time returned; she needed the weight of personal pizzas and a sleepover to return to the night, the weight of Sammy's backpack returned to her shoulders. She needed Alan to walk out of the Treasure Island again so she could tease him about his new pants and jacket and the BlackBerry still clipped to his belt. She'd loop her arm through his and maybe he wouldn't lock his arm, maybe he would loosen it and keep it there for the two-block walk to his apartment. Maybe he would say he missed her.

But just like that the night had become business. Alan was handling the night.

"No," Audrey said. She rose to her feet and wiped the grit of the sidewalk from her jeans. "I'm fine. We'll take the groceries."

Alan's fingers touched Audrey's wrist as he dropped his keys in her hand. "I'll see you there," he said. He winked at Sammy, mussed Dex's hair, and walked down Wells Street toward North Avenue. The boys and Audrey walked in silence.

At the sound of the doorbell Sammy hit the button on the intercom and spoke into the grill.

"Who's there?"

"It's your father, Sammy."

"What's the password?"

"Pizza," Alan said.

"What kind?" Sammy said.

"The kind we don't eat until I come up," Alan said, and Sammy buzzed him in.

When he walked through the door the boys were playing cards on the living room carpet. Audrey sat on the couch.

Dex looked up at him.

"No luck, Dex," he said, "but I think Sammy was right. I think you would have remembered packing Smokey. And everything else that was lost can be replaced, right?"

Dex buried the tip of a finger in the carpet. Sammy looked at Dex.

"Absolutely," Audrey said, walking into the kitchen. "We'll go back home tomorrow and I bet you a quarter Smokey will be waiting for us."

Dex bent his head toward the cards on the floor and filled his cheeks with air.

"What do you want on your pizzas?" Alan asked.

"Just cheese for me," Sammy said. He looked at Dex. "Pepperoni for Dex," and Dex nodded.

When Alan joined Audrey in the kitchen, he turned on the light above the oven and flipped the ceiling light switch to off.

"Pepperoni for Dex, cheese for Sammy, black olives for me," he said.

Audrey nodded at two bowls she'd already set aside with black olives and pepperoni. On the stove, broccoli florets steamed in a pan.

"No luck with the backpack?" Audrey said.

Alan shook his head, rinsed his hands in the sink. Flicking the water from his fingers, he looked at the handle of the refrigerator door for the dishtowel.

"I got it," Audrey said, and she tossed him the towel.

Alan wiped his hands and returned the towel to the refrigerator. "I had forgotten about Smokey," he said. "The polar bear, right?"

"Yeah," Audrey said.

Alan removed a dishcloth from the bowl of dough rising on the counter and flattened a section of it into a disc. His sleeves were cuffed to his elbows. He rubbed at an itch on his cheek with the back of his hand and peeled the flat circle of dough from the blue marble countertop. When he began to whistle "That's Amore", Sammy and Dex walked into the room and watched him twirl the dough in the air while Audrey grated the mozzarella.

"Get ready, Dex," Alan said. "This one's yours. Hands clean?"

"They're fine, Dad."

Alan sent the Frisbee of dough in the air and Dex caught it on his fist and gave it a whirl while Alan flattened a lump of dough for Sammy. Audrey flattened her own dough with the heel of her hand and soon they were all flipping and twirling discs and humming along with Alan.

When their pizzas were in the oven the boys returned to their card game in the living room. Alan shut the oven door and tossed two padded mitts to the counter.

Audrey stacked them precisely, thumb to thumb, smoothed her hand over the gloves.

"You're sure this is okay, Alan?"

"What?"

"Staying here?"

"Why wouldn't it be?"

"I don't know."

"It's fine, Audrey."

He unrolled his sleeves and buttoned them at his wrists while Audrey looked at him.

"It's fine," he said again.

Audrey filled the sink with soapy water. She knocked the cheese grater against the inside wall of Alan's garbage can, a silver tube in the corner of the kitchen, and set the grater in the sink. She poked her fingers in the warm water and stirred it in tiny circles. She wondered if Alan was looking at her.

"My nightdress was in the backpack, too," she said.

"The white one?"

Audrey nodded.

"You packed that tonight?" he said.

Audrey didn't answer. She closed her eyes at the sink. Behind her Alan set the sauce spoon in the water gently. He soaked a Handi-Wipe in the sink and squeezed it to wipe the counter.

"It was so white," he said.

Audrey wiped a swirl of hair from her face and washed the dishes.

After dinner, they played Scrabble, which Sammy said he liked better than Monopoly, anyway. Alan started the game with *twig*, to which Sammy added *Q*, *U*, and *I*, to make *quit*. Audrey peeked to her right at Dex's letters. On his shelf he'd arranged them to read *unite*; he also had an *O* and a blank tile. He set the word *quote* on the board but before he'd lined the letters neatly, he shuffled the *E* around and added the rest of his letters to form the word *quotient*.

"Thirty-two points," Dex said.

"Count again," Alan said. "You also get fifty points for using up all your letters on one turn. That just may be an insurmountable lead you've got there, Dex."

"What does *quotient* mean?" Sammy said.

"It's a math term," Audrey said. "It has something to do with division."

"It's the answer to a division problem," Dex said.

"In the history of our family that might be a Scrabble record," Alan said, and Audrey chewed on the inside of her cheek.

Throughout the game Alan cited examples of what it meant to *open the board*. Twice, he helped Sammy out when he struggled with a word. Dex refused assistance on every turn.

Afterward they watched *Mission Impossible* on the living room TV. Alan sat on the floor with his back against the couch, Dex lying against his chest. Audrey sat on the sofa next to Sammy and when she relaxed her knee it leaned against Alan's shoulder. Sammy fell asleep before the movie ended, and when Dex flinched in almost-sleep against his father's chest Alan tapped his shoulders.

"Let me up, buddy," he said, and Dex joined his brother on the other side of Audrey. They were bookends at Audrey's hips, their heads resting on sofa pillows, their legs hooked over opposite arms of the couch.

From the kitchen came the sound of a cabinet closing, came the screech of the coffee grinder.

When Alan returned he dropped two folded blankets on the floor at Audrey's feet—quilts his mother had made for the boys. They had become part of Alan's apartment. He had taken them with him.

"Blankets for the boys," he said. "I'm gonna hit the sack. Coffee's set to go if you wake up first. Just hit the switch."

Alan kissed the boys good night and flipped his hand in a kind of wave at Audrey on his way toward his room.

"'Night," he said.

Audrey nodded.

She did not watch Alan walk to his room.

While the movie played she finger-combed the boys' hair.

Blankets for the boys, he had said. What about her? Had Alan left an opening for her to join him in his bed?

When the movie ended Audrey covered Sammy and Dex with the quilts. She walked to the television and thumbed through the late night options, finally settling on the Animal Channel. She turned the volume down and watched hollow-ly for a moment. She walked to the boys' room and leaned against the frame of the doorway. The room smelled of new wood and linens. She flipped the light switch. There were the new bunk beds the boys had mentioned after their last visit. She sat on the lower bunk and brushed her hands over the sheets, striped in shades of brown, cool and papery.

And a dresser. She would not have guessed the dresser. And a mirror on the wall above it. Would Alan have thought to put a mirror in the boys' room? Or was that something only a woman would think to do? She walked to the light switch at the door and lowered it to a dimmer possibility.

She stood at the mirror, and as she pulled her hair back in a ponytail and shaped it into a bun she held in place, she felt the cloth of her shirt rise against her braless nipples. She separated wisps of her hair and swirled them in front of her ears. She smoothed her hair over her shoulders, and in front of the mirror unbuttoned her shirt. She slipped her arms from the sleeves, let her blouse fall to the floor, and covering her breasts with one arm she stepped from her jeans.

She listened for sounds from the living room—for Sammy's quick breaths, nearly two for each of Dex's.

Audrey folded her pants and set them on the dresser. She stood in her underwear in front of the mirror, and held a hand to each of her breasts. He had told her last April—or was it May?—that she still had the breasts of a girl, and now Audrey looked at them in the mirror, her girl breasts. Isabel hadn't taken to Audrey's milk on the day of her birth—which was fine; she'd always said that was fine. And when Dex was born she couldn't bear to even try.

Audrey squinted, imagining her hands were the hands of her husband smoothing across her breasts and down her body from behind. She removed her underwear, folded them into a tiny square and stacked them on her pants. Folded and stacked her shirt as well. She peeked into the living room and, walking past the boys, tiptoed toward Alan's room, grateful for the silence of the carpeted floor.

The door to his room was opened slightly. He could have closed his door but it was open. Audrey stopped at his doorway, and leaning against it she peeked inside. He slept on his stomach, his face turned away, his covers pulled to his neck. Beneath the blankets he would be wearing fresh boxers and a clean T-shirt. Audrey closed her eyes and breathed through her nose. He was still her husband.

When she opened her eyes and looked again, his head was turned toward the doorway. He had shifted in his sleep, had freed his bare right leg from under the covers. Was it possible he was naked beneath them? Perhaps he thought she might join him, perhaps he was waiting for her. Hadn't she mentioned she'd packed her white nightdress?

Audrey stepped into the doorway where the faint glow of light from the living room would have been enough for a husband to know a wife was naked at the edge of his vision. She still had the breasts of a girl. He had said that. Surely it took more than a few months to lose the breasts of a girl.

With one foot beyond the threshold she held her hand to the low arc of her left breast where her heart pounded for release. Her eyes had adjusted to the dim glow of the city lights filtered through the cloth dressings of the windows on either side of his bed. She tiptoed deeper into the room, toward the left side of his bed. After each step she stopped to determine if his breaths were the breaths of a sleeping man. When she came close enough to reach forward and touch his back, she stood still.

If their positions had been reversed, she wondered, would she have known he was there? How could she not? Even if her face had been turned away as his was now. Even if she were sleeping the dead sleep of night she would have known he was there. What was it that made possible such knowledge?

She could walk to the other side and climb in under the covers. That was an option. She was still his wife. She could face the wall and not look his way. During the night, if he learned she was next to him—naked—would that shock him? She had nothing to sleep in. He knew that. Did he expect her to sleep in her blue jeans? He could have offered her something to sleep in.

But would she sleep? Or would she lie awake and consider their nearness? How she could reach her fingers just inches away and touch him. She would will herself to sleep. She would lie there not expecting to be touched, not expecting Alan to wake and hold her, or visit her deeply. She would sleep as a wife slept.

Audrey stepped toward these recent thoughts. Beneath her weight she felt the carpeted depression of wood, heard the infinitesimal calibrations of creaking wood beneath her bare feet.

Alan shifted again. He turned his sleeping face toward Audrey who froze, who felt her blood throb, her heart pulse through her arm-crossed breasts. When he was still again, she stepped backward; uncrossing her arms, she hesitated at the footboard. She began to step toward the far side of Alan's bed but froze at a flash of movement to her left. She covered her breasts again and looked over her shoulder. It was only the mirror. Audrey naked. Hands on opposite shoulders, forearms covering her breasts. Behind her, Alan. She strained to see if his eyes were open but his face was featureless in the shadowy blue of the mirrored room, his body in the shape of sleeping. He could be watching her now, she thought: his wife standing naked at the foot of his bed.

Audrey slid her hands slowly down her body from their hold at her shoulders.

There.

In the mirror.

All of her.

Alan behind her.

Their sons asleep in the next room. *Her* sons. They had come from these hips. As had Isabel. She had seen them all come from inside her. If she closed her eyes and called upon the seven and eleven and fifteen years that had passed since their births she could still hear the sounds, still smell the smells of their egress. The boys had their own things now. They spelled words now and refused assistance, and they had come from inside her. She had given birth to three children. And had buried one. The breasts in that mirror were not the breasts of a girl, Alan. There were no girls anymore, only boys. There were boys and there was a woman, Alan! These were the breasts of a woman.

She held her arms at her sides, palms supine before her.

If she had been watching herself from the bed—if she had been watching Audrey from where Alan lay—and she saw herself now as she was, she would have sat up in bed. She would have swung her feet onto the floor and walked to herself. She would have taken herself in her arms, overwhelmed with her own beauty and with love. She would have thanked herself for having whatever it took to come into this bedroom. She would have held herself, breast against breast, felt her own heart beating against herself. She would have buried her face in her own neck and probably would have wept, would have wept so profoundly she might have awakened the boys. Or she might have awakened something else, something so deep inside her that its awakening might have been terrible, might have been beautiful.

Holding her arms out like a child pretending flight, Audrey looked down and stepped back to see the prints her feet had made, the easy V of her feet pressed into the carpet. She stepped back into the prints and began inching her feet in slow, clockwise quarter-steps. And in this way, facing the mirror and then the window and then Alan and then the doorway, through separate quarters of her journey, she twirled a slow and silent twirl. And in the mirror she watched herself; even with her back to the mirror she watched herself, strained to see all of her slowly twirling self, the shape of Alan somewhere behind her. And if her husband had opened his eyes then he would have seen the figure of his naked and slowly spinning wife, her face smiling and wet with tears, skin flush with the blood she sent to each living cell of her September skin, her flesh warm and damp with the sweat of dozens of twirlings. And when Audrey finally stopped, she faced the doorway and smiled. She did not look back at her sleeping husband. She set her hands at her sides and stepped toward the doorway, leaving behind her the impression of a circle, its rim the length of her feet.

In the hallway, she wiped her eyes with her fingers. She leaned against the cool paint of the wall until her tears dried on her hands and she walked toward the living room.

On the sofa, Dex and Sammy were still bookends, their heads toward the center of the couch, the space from which she had watched *Mission Impossible* still open. Naked, she stood there. She had tiptoed past them on her way to Alan's room, fully aware of her nakedness in their clothed and sleeping presence. But what was there to be ashamed of? They had come from her.

Audrey took her place between them once again. On the Animal Channel a frog's tongue darted out in slow motion and thwacked a hapless lightning bug. The gullet of the frog glowed orange with the last luminescence of the summer insect. To Audrey's right, she ran her fingers through Dex's hair. To her left, Sammy's.

Soon she would rise from the couch and turn off the television. She would sleep in the lower bunk and in the morning would wake before everyone. She would not hit the switch on Alan's new coffeemaker. Alan would not wake to its sweet, throaty hissings, nor to the kitchened rills of coffee steam.

In the morning she would go to the Starbuck's on North and Wells and order a grande cup of the day, and on her way back to Alan's to get the boys, she would take the alleys and look for Sammy's backpack. She was certain she would not find the Game Boys. Nor would she find her glasses. She suspected such things were currency in the alleys of the city. Even the playing cards would be gone. She hoped not to find the other things, but feared she would. She would weep, or churn with anger, to see Sammy's backpack in the alley, to see the nightdress, to see the boys' pants and boxer shorts, to see their pajamas and socks discovered to the world like family photos scattered along the alleys and atop the lids of garbage cans. Piece by piece she would collect them. She would gather their things and put them into the shell of the backpack, crying and cursing at the capacity of man, and she would dump the whole mess into a garbage can.

Audrey stood and leaned to kiss the boys good night. She turned off the television and waited while its light collapsed into a tiny pinprick of electricity in the middle of the dark box, and there she stood until she saw the reflected shapes of her sons on the screen.

In the boys' room she turned the dimmer off. She set her stack of clothes on the floor at the bedside of the lower bunk and peeled the flat sheet away from the fitted sheet, slipping between them. The bed was cool against her back. She felt the fresh zephyr of the flat sheet as it fell cool and papery over her. She lifted the sheet to feel its breeze once more, and when she released her fingers from the hem of the sheet it floated like a whisper to her body, settling around her feet, her legs, and in what space she left open between them. It came to rest around her hips like a cool shadow and settled about her breasts like a kiss.

She considered then, the image of her nightdress in the alley—the startling white of it against whatever color the city would muster on a September morning. She imagined Smokey as well. Hopefully he was tucked in under the blankets at home, but if he was crammed between garbage cans or sitting against a telephone pole or lying in a puddle in the alley she would pick him up, too. She would bury him. She would hide all of their history beneath the detritus of the city and tell the boys she hadn't found a thing. She would tell them the backpack and everything in it was no longer theirs. What things could be replaced, they would replace. They would buy another Monopoly game. Or Scrabble. They would get new pajamas and boxers, new toothbrushes. They would start over.

And linens, too. She would get new linens tomorrow.

CHAPTER 4

Descending Man
(August 2007)

To lock the exterior door of the apartment in Chicago, Audrey had to grimace and yank the handle and turn the key simultaneously. It usually worked on the first effort, but in the August heat the door swelled and the spring paint softened on the swollen wood and at the third attempt it took all of Audrey's strength to refrain from swearing at the door in the presence of the boys. On the fourth attempt the door finally locked.

She would not catch up to Dex and Sammy until she reached her car where they waited for her, still comparing notes from their respective conversations with their father about his work.

Dex was reminding Sammy of the time their father had seen a man at Cook County Hospital walk into the trauma unit carrying his own intestines in his hands. Earlier that afternoon the boys made a list from memory of the ten most violent corners in Chicago.

It was still hard to believe it was Alan they were talking about. Four short years before, he was an animal behavior research scientist and now—somehow—he was an attorney tracking violent crimes for the Chicago Police Department. Now he was picking up his shirts medium starched from the cleaners. Now he was wearing a BlackBerry clipped to his pleated pants.

Audrey was still Audrey. She still wore unpressed pants and shirts right out of the dryer. She still taught English at Francis Parker School, still insisted on the precision of words and gestured like a lefty, shaping ideas in her hand with her fingers spread and curved as though her thoughts were invisible cantaloupes, things you could hold.

It was to their credit, Audrey thought as she pulled onto the Eisenhower Expressway, that Alan and she still did things together. As a family, more or less. She thought the same thing again, after a dinner of grilled cheeseburgers at Alan's place, when they left his apartment for a long walk to Oak Park for ice cream.

It was Audrey's idea, the ice cream. Before the night was through, she would remind herself a number of times that the walk to the Hole-in-the-Wall was her idea. "Let's get chocolate and vanilla swirl ice-cream cones from the Hole-in-the-Wall," she had said. And everyone agreed that it was an excellent idea.

While they were walking to the Hole-in-the-Wall, though, on the corner of Garfield and Clinton—just blocks from their destination—a shoeless man wearing a Boston Red Sox baseball cap, fell, or jumped, from the fourth or fifth floor ledge of an apartment building across the street from the highway.

Later, as they walked home, Dex, who was twelve, said that it was the fourth floor from which the man fell or jumped, but Sammy, who was eight, said it was the fifth.

"He wouldn't have died if it was only the fourth floor, Dex."

"How do you know?"

"I just know," Sammy said.

"I *saw* the man fall," Dex said. "Did you *see* the man fall?"

"Yes, I did."

"You may have seen him as he was *falling*," Dex said. "But I saw him *fall*. Okay? Did you see him fall?"

Neither Audrey nor Alan saw the man fall or jump. Much later, Audrey took to using *descend* as the verb for what the man did.

They turned, Audrey and Alan, at the sound of the body hitting the sidewalk. Later, at Alan's apartment, Audrey paused—was deliberate—as she attempted to put words to the sound of the man hitting the ground. She held her invisible cantaloupe in her left hand.

"It didn't sound like how I thought a body hitting a sidewalk would sound," she said. "I don't know. I expected something . . ." She pumped the back of her arm against her thigh. "Something different. It was nothing like what I thought it might be. It was the sound of a wooden box wrapped in a blanket crashing onto something made of steel. The top of a car maybe."

"Maybe a skateboard falling on a car," she said later.

And then, as though nailing the exact sound—as though putting the perfect words to the sound that played over in her head —was the thing she most needed to do in order to make it go away, she tried once again to describe it to Alan.

"It sounded," she said, "like the clattering of bones inside a bag of skin."

But she was not happy with this simile, even as she dragged it to the surface; it was much too close to the actual thing. That's what her students did, used similes that were too much like the thing they were meant to describe. But Audrey grew still after she hit upon that flawed simile—and silent, as though it were the closest thing to true that she would ever find.

"That's all we are, Alan, isn't it?" she said. "Bones? Inside bags of skin?"

The boys were walking behind Alan and Audrey when it happened. They had just crossed Wisconsin Street on their way to the ice cream shop when Dex saw the man on the ledge. He was wearing a baseball cap and drinking from something in a green bottle. Dex watched the man on the ledge for three blocks while Sammy was explaining why sour cherries were not only the best candy made at the Ferrara Pan candy factory, but they were the best candy ever.

Audrey's left hand was in the shape of a point she was making to Alan about food, or rather about the annoyance of having to eat so often, when, at the instant of the explosion of something like a wooden box on the sidewalk across the street, she turned back to her children and held her arms out as an instinctive shield in front of them; she turned so quickly to locate them it seemed more a flinching than anything else, and when she saw them standing safe at the curb staring at something across the street, she finally turned toward the sound. Which was when she saw the man. He wore a baseball cap. In his hand was a Heineken bottle, unbroken and upright. One leg was twisted wrongly beneath him and the heel of that shoeless foot rested on his right shoulder. The other foot—Audrey could not tell which was the right and which the left—was set, casual and flat, on the ground. It was also unshod, and his knee was raised like a man reading a book just before taking a nap on a couch. He was dead.

Instantly—from the way Dex and Sammy hadn't jumped at the sound, and from their frozen silence—Audrey was certain the boys had seen him fall. When she looked back again at Alan he was staring at the man. In the presence of their children he was staring from the man's head to his twisted legs and feet, and even as Audrey screamed, "What are you doing, Alan? What the hell are you looking at?" she knew her anger was not meant for him—not completely—but was meant for the thing the boys had seen. Or for herself. For not being able to protect them from seeing such a thing.

There was nothing else to scream at, though. She couldn't scream at her children: boys could not be faulted for staring at a dead man. Alan was the only thing she could scream at, she could punch.

She had been talking about food. This is what she kept saying to Alan on the way to his apartment afterward.

"I was talking about food," she kept saying to Alan. "While our sons were watching a man fall from a building, I was talking about food."

While they sat on the cement stair of the corner storefront next door to the Hole-in-the-Wall, Alan pointed to the long line in front of the ice cream shop and mentioned how lucky they were to have beaten the rush, and Audrey glared at him.

"What?" Alan said.

"Did you really just say that?" she said.

"What?" Alan said again. "I'm just saying."

The boys sat to Alan's left. Sammy licked a full loop around the melting base of ice cream along the rim of his cone. Dex watched him. Audrey did not have an ice-cream cone, though the idea of the walk had been hers.

When Sammy stopped licking his ice-cream cone, he looked up to see Dex staring at him.

"Did you really see him fall, Dex?" Sammy said.

Dex nodded.

"Swear to God?"

"Swear to God," Dex said.

"Then why didn't you tell me," Sammy said.

Dex licked his ice-cream cone.

"If you saw him up there," Sammy said, "why didn't you tell me?"

Audrey rubbed her temples.

"Because I thought he was going to fall."

Audrey pressed her fingers into the back of her neck.

"But why didn't you tell me?" Sammy said.

"Because I didn't want you to see him fall, okay?" Dex said.

"Shut up," Audrey said.

Sammy flinched.

"Don't you get it?" Dex said.

"Shut up!" Audrey said again, and the boys fell silent.

A woman in line at the Hole-in-the-Wall stopped talking and looked toward the corner. Behind her, two girls in their teens looked at Audrey and then looked away.

Sammy leaned against Alan's shoulder. Dex looked up at his father and shrugged an apology, as though it were his father whom he had wronged. As though it were his fault that his mother had just been replaced by a strange woman. Alan put his hand up and pressed the space between him and the boys as if to soften the thing that Audrey had done. He switched his ice-cream cone to his left hand and put his right hand on Audrey's shoulder.

It was the first time he had touched her since he had moved out in May of the previous year. Fifteen months.

"I'm sorry," Audrey said.

"It's okay, Mom," Sammy said.

"It's fine," Dex said.

"No, it's not," Audrey said.

Sammy said, "Could we stay at your place tonight, Dad?"

And Dex said, "Yeah, Dad. Could we?"

And Audrey began to cry.

"Yes," Alan said. "You can all stay tonight."

On their way back to Alan's house they walked westward up Harrison Street, on the other side of the highway. Dex and Sammy walked in front and spoke quietly. When Sammy looked back he seemed relieved that Alan and Audrey were still there, and when Dex looked back he seemed to be gauging the distance between them, seemed to be considering distance and sound.

When they reached the Ferrara Pan candy factory at the south end of the Circle Bridge, Dex stopped and held up his arm for all of them to stop and determine the products that had been made that day. He closed his eyes and raised his nose to the sky to sniff at the air. Sammy did the same then, and Audrey and Alan followed.

"Dad?" Dex said. "You first."

"Fruit Stripes bubble gum," Alan said.

"Mom?"

"Boston Baked Beans," she said.

"Sammy?" Dex said.

"I was going to say Fruit Stripes," Sammy said.

"Pick another," Dex said, and Sammy sniffed again.

"Lemon Heads," Sammy said.

"Well done," Dex said, sniffing again. "That's about it."

When they started up the bridge to get to Alan's apartment they had arranged themselves into new pairings.

Audrey and Dex trailed behind Sammy and Alan on the narrow walkway of the Circle Bridge. Audrey had her arm hooked in Dex's. In front of them Sammy pointed at tall things—houses, billboards, factory smokestacks, trees, streetlights—and asked his father, after each object was pointed out, if a man could die if he fell from there, if he fell from there, from there.

At the top of the bridge, Dex held his hand out for Audrey to stop while Sammy and Alan walked ahead. Audrey wondered then if Dex, too, had heard Sammy asking Alan about the heights of things.

"What is it, sweetie?" Audrey said.

Dex pointed to a line of trees past the bottom of the hill at the corner of Jackson and Circle.

"Do you see those trees, Mom?" he said.

"Where?" Audrey said.

"In front of Dad's apartment."

"Yes," she said. "What about them?"

"They're ginkgo trees," Dex said. He licked his finger and raised it in the air above his shoulder. "There isn't much of a wind tonight, is there?" he said.

"There's a little bit," Audrey said. "Why do you ask?"

"When we're in the bunk beds in our bedroom at Dad's, and the wind blows in the summer, the leaves of the ginkgo trees sound like a million tiny hands clapping." Dex smiled. "Like babies' hands."

Audrey smiled.

"That's beautiful, Dex," she said. "That's a thing that could never be recorded, a million babies clapping hands."

"I know," Dex said. And they walked down Circle Bridge, she with her arm across his shoulder.

Together, Alan and Audrey tucked the boys into their bunk beds, and together they kissed the boys good night. Afterward, sitting on stools at the island in the center of Alan's kitchen, they had glasses of red wine. Mostly in silence they had them. Alan would have liked all of the night to be in silence, it seemed, but Audrey continued to break the quiet; she could not put a stop to the words about the final sounds and the sights of the fallen man.

"Can we talk about something else?" Alan said.

And Audrey would sit for a while in a quiet she could not sustain for long.

She talked about how the man was barefoot.

"I guess I was thinking how he should have had shoes on. Do you think he had been sitting on the ledge or the roof without shoes?" she said. "There's this phenomenon of people jumping out of their shoes in moments of great fear or tragedy," she said. "Maybe it was that."

She spoke in fragments, as though to piece the event together into solid and definite memory.

"He was wearing shorts, too. It was a warm beautiful day today, wasn't it, Alan? Why do I think it would not have been so bad if he had pants on?" she said.

"Damn," she said. "He should've been covered up."

"Please," Alan said.

And Audrey grew quiet again.

In the ephemeral silence, Audrey heard sounds coming from the boys' room. She nodded toward them and looked at Alan.

"And now they have this," she said.

"Now they have what?" Alan said.

"This night," Audrey said. "Now they have this night to remember."

"Audrey," he said. "Can you please give it a rest?"

She leaned toward Alan as though he had asked to meet her halfway for a kiss.

"Fuck you, Alan," she whispered. "Fuck you, okay?"

She returned to her space at the island and then spoke as if to her own glass of wine. "I don't want to give it a rest anymore, Alan. That's all I've been doing for three years, letting it rest."

She sipped from her glass and leaned toward the boys' room to listen for them again.

"I'm sorry, Alan," she said. "Maybe you see this stuff every day, but I don't. I have to talk about it."

She was quiet for a long while then, but when she remembered what she told the boys at the Hole-in-the-Wall she began to cry again. Alan did not put his hand to her back.

"I told them to shut up, Alan," she said. "I promised I would never do that."

And as she sat on the stool at the island in the kitchen she put her face in her hands and sobbed.

When she stopped, Audrey shaped her left hand into a definite hold on some unseen thing in the kitchen air and said, "And you were eating ice cream on the corner like you had not just seen a dead man on the sidewalk. Jesus, Alan."

It was then that the boys' sibilant whispers snaked into the kitchen and put a stop to Audrey's words.

She inched toward their bedroom and Alan put his fingers to the crook of her arm.

"Let them talk," he said, and Audrey pulled her arm away.

"I want to hear them," she said, and she walked toward their room. She stood hidden by the wall that separated their room from the rest of the house, and she listened.

"I *did* see him," Sammy said.

"No, you didn't."

"Yes I did," Sammy said.

"No, you didn't, Sammy," Dex said. "Stop lying."

"I'm not lying," Sammy said.

"Shut up," Dex said.

Audrey flinched at the sound of her words in Dex's voice. She put her hands to her own mouth.

"Don't tell me to shut up," Sammy said. "I saw him, and he didn't make like he was falling. He didn't try to grab on to anything like you do if you're about to fall."

The boys were quiet then.

Audrey held her hand to her mouth to keep it from crying or speaking or anything else a mouth might do to betray a mother. And then Dex spoke.

"If you did see him, Sammy. Then what were you thinking?"

There was no response from Sammy.

"What were you thinking when the man was falling?" Dex said.

"I'm not going to tell you," Sammy said, and Dex asked again.

"Tell me," Dex said. "What was going through your head when you saw the man fall?"

Audrey looked into the kitchen. Alan, sitting over his glass of wine and thumbing some message into his BlackBerry.

"What were you thinking, Sammy?" Dex said.

"I don't know," Sammy said. "Nothing."

A breeze floated through the open windows of Alan's second-floor apartment and billowed the hem of the curtains into the living room like a whisper.

"I wish today never happened," Dex said.

"Me, too," Sammy said.

Another breeze trembled through the leaves of the ginkgo trees.

"Let's pretend it didn't," Sammy said.

Audrey looked out onto the fan-shaped leaves of the ginkgo trees and turned an ear to the window.

"Okay," Dex said.

Outside their room Audrey closed her eyes and listened. It *was* like clapping. Like a million, tiny, clapping hands.

CHAPTER 5

The White Rose of Chicago
(October 2007)

When Audrey boarded the bus at Clark and North Avenue she had a bag from the frame store in her hands. Inside the bag was a print by an artist named Fitzpatrick protected with cardboard and wrapped in brown paper. She dropped her change in the fare box and smiled at the bus driver, a woman with brown hair that was too long for her. It seemed to Audrey as though the woman was trying to make some kind of point with her hair, as though that was her thing, to have long hair—as though she had made a promise when she was young that she would never cut her hair. As though her hair was a promise to keep.

As she walked past the driver Audrey thought that if she were to say everything that crossed her mind, she would tell the bus driver this: Your hair is too long. You should cut it. You would look better with short hair. But Audrey did not say everything that crossed her mind. There were things that crossed her mind that she never mentioned.

On Audrey's right, in the first pair of seats facing the front of the bus, an old woman sat with her hands folded daintily on her lap. She was a skinny black woman. She looked fragile and sweet and wore a spring hat. It was October, but Audrey thought the old woman's hat was a perfect hat for the spring.

The seat next to the old woman was empty. It seemed to Audrey that the seat was maybe four long strides from the rear exit, four long strides from the front.

The black woman smiled and Audrey sat in the empty seat next to her as the bus pulled into the intersection at the change of the light from red to green and eased into the Clark Street traffic.

Audrey felt the old woman look at her bag and then up at Audrey twice in the span of the next block. The old woman patted the back of one of her brown hands with the palm of the other—gently, three times—as if one of her hands were considering conversing with Audrey, and the other hand were advising against it. Before the old woman spoke, she patted her hand once more.

"You about to hang something on your living room wall, ain't you?" the old woman said to Audrey.

"I beg your pardon?" Audrey said.

"I said, you fixing to hang something on your wall?"

"Oh, yes," Audrey said.

The woman nodded and patted her hand as if to congratulate herself for having properly guessed some secret thing about Audrey.

Audrey pictured the narrow rectangle of wall space between the windows in the kitchen where the drawing would go. Natural light drenched the room from noon until dusk. She imagined sitting at the wrought-iron table in the kitchen with the picture over her shoulder.

"I known it must be something special," the skinny woman said. "It's wrapped up so precious."

Audrey considered saying something more, but she only nodded and brushed her fingers along the outside of the bag.

The old woman patted her own hand again and nodded. "Yes, ma'am," she said. "I known it must be something precious."

Audrey smiled and spoke. "It's called the White Rose of Chicago," she said. "It's a print of a drawing collage."

Audrey called upon the central image of the print, the face of a woman growing from the heart of a white rose. She did not recite the words that stood like an untrustworthy tower down the left side of the collage, but she could have recited them. She had them memorized. She rolled them silently in her mouth while air hissed from the brakes of the bus at LaSalle.

the
flowers
own
her;
fingers,
petals,
hands
and lips.
She is
dressed
in the
logic
of a
white
flower.
She
touches
the small
of your

back while
you shave
and you
begin to
shake and
turn as white
as the statue
of her
ghosts.

Audrey thought that if pressed by the old woman to show her the print, she would; if pressed to read its poetry aloud, she might do that as well.

"I guess I don't know so much about art," the woman said. "Least that's what my daughter tells me."

The old woman quick-laughed through her nose and patted her own hand.

"Came home with a painting and tacked up a nail in the middle of the wall and made me close my eyes while she hung it up there, and so I closed my eyes and waited there with my eyes closed, and then my daughter said, 'Okay, Mama. Now when you open your eyes, I want you to look at this painting but don't say nothing about it right away. Just look at it for a while before you say something.' And when I opened my eyes up, there in the middle of my living room was a picture of four black children with they heads cut off."

The old woman shook her head slowly and smiled as though she were still trying to figure out what beauty her daughter might have seen in the painting she had tacked up on the old woman's wall. Audrey's smile was closer to a laugh than a smile, and in the presence of it, the old woman seemed animated.

"And I said to her, I said, 'You just let me know when

I can say something about that picture, child."

The old woman crossed her arms as though she were back in her living room looking at the painting, then she continued.

"'Okay, Mama,' she said. 'Tell me what you think about that.' And I said, 'Well, child, that there picture that you put up on my living room wall is a picture of four little chocolate children, ain't got no heads.' And she said, 'Mama, don't you see? That's the whole point. You don't know nothin' about art, do you? That's a *statement* the artist trying to make.'"

The old woman shook her head slowly and laughed. She patted her hand on her lap. Audrey smiled.

"She may be right," the old woman said. "I may not know nothin' about art. But she asked me what I thought about it and that's what I told her. It's still up there, that old picture," the woman said.

Two blocks passed before the old woman spoke again.

Across the black rubber walkway from them, a woman with a massive chest and square face sat with a lime green bucket in the seat next to her. She had a short haircut and a sweater that was tiny on her, unbuttonable across her chest. Audrey made out the form of a brush and rags through the translucent pail. Audrey thought the woman might have been Polish. Her fingers were locked together across her chest as though it was the only way they could keep from falling to her side. Her hands were rough.

At Wisconsin Street, a pale hulk of a man boarded the bus. He reminded Audrey of Lenny from *Of Mice and Men*. He wore short pants, and blue veins vivid as atlas rivers branched across his legs. He was fleshy.

Something was wrong with the man. His lower lip was twice the size of his upper lip. His head tilted downward and his mouth hung open as though his lower lip was too heavy for the rest of him, as though his lip was to blame for the tilt of his head and his lumbering gait.

He carried a cane, but it seemed as though he had some ill-formed notion of how to use it. He wore thick eyeglasses. He was ugly in every way, Audrey thought—his skin, his face, his size—but in his face he was a child.

He had a leather change purse that a woman might use; in his hands it looked as small as a prune.

The man clinked his change into the fare box. There were two spaces open on the bench facing the aisle in front of the cleaning lady, but the large man did not sit down. He leaned against the pole in front of the open seats and faced the back of the bus. Like a man who was trying to look cool, Audrey thought.

When the bus jerked forward, it seemed for a moment that the man was about to fall. Audrey flinched in her seat toward him, but the man reached up and grasped the support bar in time to catch himself, and Audrey resettled into her seat.

The old woman patted her hand again.

"How old are your children?" she asked Audrey.

"I'm sorry?" Audrey said.

"Your children," the old woman said. "How old are they?"

"Thirteen and nine," Audrey said.

"I knowed you had children by the way you started toward the man," the old woman said.

"Yes," Audrey said. "Two boys." And the old woman nodded.

Audrey did not tell the old woman that she'd had a daughter once as well. That her name was Isabel and that she had disappeared on a summer night three years before. That she would have been eighteen now. She did not tell the old woman that it had been three years since Audrey had said her daughter's name aloud.

In front of her, the hulking man held his cane in the

squeeze of his upper arm against his side. His change purse was still open and he was smiling stupidly and poking his finger through his coins.

Even the seated passengers were nearly thrown from their seats when the long-haired bus driver slammed her black-shod foot on the brakes to keep from hitting a boy on a bicycle outside. When the bus jerked to a stop the big man fell backward with a blow that shook the bus like an aftershock. The man's back slammed against the flat side of the fare box with a massive sound that Audrey knew—even in that instant—she would never forget. She knew immediately that she would think of that sound whenever she set her eyes on a fare box, or even thought of one: a sound a body should not make no matter the thing smashed into. With the violent thud of his huge body against the box and the clang of collected metal within there was the tinny, peppering clink of coins falling everywhere. The man was not done falling. As the bus trembled to a stop, his hulking body caromed off the side of the fare box and tumbled down the front steps of the bus. He landed with his back against the door and his feet in the air. There was the silence of post-chaos. There was change everywhere.

The old woman next to Audrey sat taller in her seat and reached around like a mother. She reached around Audrey, pressed Audrey against her own tiny frame.

Audrey wondered at the woman's instinct to hug her. In the hold of her skinny arms she wondered if she, Audrey, had said something, if she had gasped or cursed, or if she had blurted out some unintended thing that prompted the woman to hold her. She wondered if the woman sensed Audrey's need to be held in that moment, or if it was the old woman who needed something to hold. She wished Alan, her husband, were there. He knew what to do in situations like this. He would manage the chaos. See to the business of it. She would call him at work and tell him the story of the man on the bus. *We were all saying the dumbest things*, she would say. *I can't remember them now, but it seemed they were dumb things to say.*

On the bus, what Audrey was saying was "Oh my god, oh my god, oh my god." Like a desperate sinner she repeated the echoing prayer and repeated it again. But in the same moment she found herself wishing that Alan had been there, a young woman wearing a white dress—younger than Audrey by perhaps twenty years or more—ran to the front of the bus.

Audrey would remember that moment in slow motion. On the phone that evening, she would tell Alan the girl was gorgeous. *Maybe the most beautiful girl I have ever seen*, she would tell Alan. *She was gorgeous and strong. She was a woman of the prairie, Alan, a pioneer woman, and she came running to the front of the bus, and she crouched down to tend to the fallen man like a hero.*

"Can you feel your feet?" the woman in the white dress said.

"I'm all right," the man said.

"Can you feel your feet?" the woman said again.

"I'm not hurt," the man repeated.

The woman in the white dress scolded him then. She was bent over his feet. She was beautiful, Audrey was thinking. She was like an old-world mother.

"I am not asking you if you are in pain," the girl in white said. She was yelling now. "I am asking you if you can feel your feet."

"Yes," the man finally said. "I think I can feel my feet."

Behind the woman in white, the bus driver stood. "Can we lift him up?"

The woman in the white dress turned around toward

the bus driver and then looked at Audrey; she looked in Audrey's eyes, and Audrey's heart pounded behind her breast like a thing that wanted release.

"I'm not hurt," the man said again. "I'm not hurt."

Audrey stood and looked over her shoulder at the riders behind her; she had noticed none of them until that moment. There was a white man in his early thirties, wearing cargo pants and a T-shirt, and behind him a young Hispanic man—a boy, really, maybe eighteen. A woman with a tiny cell phone at her ear sat low in her seat behind them both.

"You," Audrey said, pointing to the white man, "and you," she said, turning to the other man. "Help pick this guy up."

The men looked at each other but didn't move from their seats.

"A little help, here!" Audrey yelled. "Go out the side door. Now. Help get this guy to his feet from the other side!"

Her own voice surprised her. She was aware in that moment that she wanted the woman in the white dress to be pleased with her.

The men rose from their seats like recalcitrant children and walked through the side door, and when they arrived at the front of the bus, the driver reached for the handle to open the door.

"Slowly," the woman in white said, and the bus driver inched the door open to keep the man from falling to the street below.

While the girl in white and the bus driver pulled the big man by his hands and the men from the back of the bus lifted him from the hollows of his arms, the cleaning lady and the old woman helped Audrey collect the scattered coins, and by the time the man was standing upright in the aisle, the woman in white had returned to her seat near the rear of the bus. Audrey could not recall seeing the woman walk past her.

The man held out his hand to the old woman who cupped the collected coins in her hat.

"Give me the coin purse," the old woman said. "I'll see to the coins."

As the bus driver spoke to the man, the man did not take his eyes from the old woman.

"Are you all right?" the bus driver asked the big man.

"Yes, I'm fine," the man said.

"Do you want me to call an ambulance?" the driver said.

"No, I'm fine."

"Is your head hurt?" she asked.

"No, my head is fine," the man said. He sat down in one of the seats that were still unoccupied, and the bus moved forward. Carefully, it seemed.

The old woman placed the filled coin purse in the man's hand and returned to her seat.

"He should've just sat down on that seat," the black woman said to Audrey. "They was two empty seats, right there. He should've just sat down on one of them."

In the mirror above the fare box, the bus driver looked back at the man who had fallen, and the black woman spoke again.

"And they ought to be seatbelts on buses," the woman said. "They ought to be seatbelts."

And instead of saying what had crossed her mind, Audrey only nodded. For Audrey no longer believed in seatbelts. Audrey no longer buckled her seatbelt even in her own car, and mostly she didn't mind whether the boys did or not. It was not so much the danger of accidents that worried her, as it was the danger of men.

The old woman asked Audrey about her sons then, and Audrey told her their names were Dex and Sammy, and that they were great kids, and when Audrey was certain the woman was done talking for the moment, she looked over her shoulder enough to see the woman in the white dress. She held her index finger at her lips, pressed it there, and rested her thumb at the soft underside of her chin, as though trying not to cry. As if to lock in sound. She stared out the window.

Audrey turned to the old woman next to her and spoke in a whisper.

"It would have made my sons sad to see that man fall," Audrey said, and the old woman nodded her head certainly.

"Oh, yes," she said, and she reached toward Audrey's lap and put her brown hand on Audrey's and tapped it twice.

At Belden Avenue, the huge man with the child's face stood again and leaned against the pole facing the back, as though he had already forgotten what it meant to fall hard, already forgotten the sound of his back pounding against the fare box, the sound of coins clinking everywhere.

Together, the passengers in the front of the bus— Audrey, the cleaning lady, and the old black woman—told the man to sit down.

The man returned to his seat, and the women looked at each other, shaking their heads and pressing their shoulders back, aware, all of them, that it was the man's good fortune they were present.

The bus continued several blocks without picking up or dropping off passengers, and in that long, narrow, and silent space Audrey wished she were a person who could stand up and walk to the back of the bus, hand a package to a woman in a white dress and say, *Here. This is for you. I did not know this until now, but I bought this print for you.*

When the bus angled to a stop at Arlington Place, it opened its doors to two women wearing black. They stepped toward the bus, tenderly it seemed. As though some great misfortune had led them to ascend the steps of this machine. They held their hands out as though they did not want to touch even their own luggage, which they had stacked on wheeled carriers. The woman in front turned her head slowly, as though to work with the easy breeze in a way that would not affect the part in her hair.

Audrey realized then, that she did not want the ridership of the bus to change. Not in this way. And it was clear, when she looked to her right at the cleaning lady and to her left at the old woman, that she was not alone in this. Her companions crossed their arms and set their jaws like sentinels at the gate of some special place.

The woman in front climbed onto the first step and, facing the sidewalk, she climbed another, banging her luggage against the lower stairs. She wore boots of leopard print suede. She lifted the wheels of the carrier off the ground but could not raise the thing higher. She grunted and glared at her friend on the sidewalk as though the day had suddenly slipped beyond her control. She sighed heavily and looked over her shoulder at the bus driver.

"Do you think maybe you can lower the bus for us to get on?" she said. "You can see I'm struggling here."

Audrey thought she could feel the adrenaline of the old woman next to her throb in the energy field about her skinny body. She imagined the old woman rising and putting her dukes up to fight the new riders if she had to. The Polish woman locked her eyes severely on the woman and then looked back at Audrey, confident of the solidarity between them.

"No," the bus driver said. "I will not lower the bus for you." And the woman grunted again and looked at her companion on the curb.

"Do you want to take a cab?" she said.

"Yes," the woman on the curb said. "Let's take a cab."

"Excellent idea," the bus driver said. "Excellent."

And as the bus pulled away from the sidewalk, Audrey felt the old woman's eyes on her, felt the eyes of the cleaning lady as well.

The bus made sounds of breathing, but otherwise they rode in silence.

At Diversey, the old woman stood from her seat and Audrey smiled, shifted her legs toward the aisle to allow her berth. Audrey watched her walk carefully to the front of the bus holding the support poles as she moved.

"Diversey, please," she said to the driver.

And when the bus stopped, the old woman looked at the driver and said, "Thank you, sister."

"You're welcome," the bus driver said, and she pulled the handle to open the door.

Outside, the old woman stood in the frame of the bus shelter and looked through the window at Audrey and smiled.

Audrey had planned to just smile at the old woman, thought she might even wave, but without thinking she looked at the old woman, lifted the heel of her hand to her lips, and blew the woman a kiss. The old woman laughed. When the bus pulled away, Audrey laughed as well—at the silliness of it. She had blown the old woman a kiss! Audrey wondered what Alan would say.

Behind her then, someone pulled the plastic-coated wire to call for the next stop. Without looking, Audrey knew it was the woman in white who had pulled the cord. She closed her eyes and hoped, hoped hard, that the girl would exit through the front doors of the bus and not the back. She wanted the girl to pass her as she walked up the aisle toward the front exit so that she might see her again.

But even as she hoped this, Audrey knew that walking past would not be enough. What she wanted was the girl in white to take the seat next to her, where the old black woman had been. Audrey wished she would sit next to her so that she might put her arm around the prairie girl's shoulder. She was certain the girl in the white dress would know exactly what to do. She would lean her head against Audrey, and Audrey would smooth her fingers over the girl's eyes to close them. She would comb her fingers through the girl's hair.

And when the bus came to the end of the line at Howard, when the driver said into the microphone, *Howard Street. End of the line*, Audrey would tell the bus driver girl with the long brown hair to just drive.

Just

keep

driving.

CHAPTER 6

How to Hold a Woman
(March 2008)

When they pulled into the parking space as close to the Guitar Center as they could, Audrey reached toward the floor of the passenger side at Sammy's feet and pulled her wallet from her purse, then turned to Dex in the backseat.

"You sure you don't want to come with?" she said.

"Positive," Dex said.

"You'll be all right?"

"I'll be fine, Mom."

Audrey turned again and sat with both hands on the steering wheel, breathed deeply, and adjusted the rearview mirror so she could see Dex.

"Keep the doors locked until we're back," she said, and she sat there as though she were waiting for something more than a promise that he would.

"Mom." He pointed toward the store. "You'll be able to see me in the car from the Guitar Center," he said. "I'll be fine."

"Okay," she said.

Audrey left the car and locked her door. She lifted the handle twice to make certain it was locked. She stepped toward the Guitar Center, then, but turned back once more and walked to Dex's window. When he looked up, Audrey pressed her thumb in the air.

The round muffle of her words reached him like the words of a dream.

"Please, Dex," she said. "Lock the doors."

"I will...Mom."

He thought for a moment that she caught the hesitation in his voice before he said *Mom*. She might have interpreted it as fear; it would have been enough to make her change her mind and force him to come into the Guitar Center with them.

But it was not fear. Dex had almost called her *Audrey*.

Soon after their father left, Dex and Sammy had started referring to their mother as Audrey whenever she fell into one of her moods. Lately her moods were made of worry and regret and anger and tissues, and watching his mother now—the car door closed, her head swiveling back to Dex and then ahead to locate Sammy walking toward the Guitar Center—on the edge of crying for no reason, it was clear that *Audrey* had returned. One of her hands seemed almost to be reaching toward Sammy and the store and the other back toward Dex as though she were being pulled from both ends by giant rubber bands. She put her hand to her mouth finally and turned from Dex, nearly running toward Sammy and two thousand guitars U-hooked to the walls of the giant store. Everything was so fucking dramatic.

That was the other thing. On Wednesday of that week the boys had begun to swear. They were sitting on the swings in Circle Park across the street from their father's apartment, waiting for Audrey to pick them up when Dex thought of the swearing idea.

"Who do you think will pick us up today?" Dex had said. "Mom or Audrey?"

"I think Mom," Sammy said.

"I think Audrey," Dex said.

Sammy was twisting absently on the black rubber swing when a cyclist riding past swore at the driver of a yellow sport utility vehicle for driving too close to the sidewalk. He looked up at the sound of Dex laughing.

"What's so funny?" Sammy said.

"Sometimes I wish I could just swear," Dex said. "It makes me laugh to hear swearing like that."

Sammy smiled and let the swing tick to a stop. He locked his fingers together and looked at the crooks of his arms where the cold links of the swing chain seemed threaded through his skin.

"Would you snitch on me if I swore?" Dex said.

"What do you mean?" Sammy said.

"I mean if I swore," Dex said, "would you tell on me and make Audrey freak out?"

"No," Sammy said. "I wouldn't snitch." Sammy was toeing a tiny valley into the new blanket of cedar chips at his feet.

"What do you say we both start swearing, then?" Dex said.

"What do you mean?" Sammy said.

"I mean we should both swear," Dex said, and Sammy smiled crookedly.

He looked up at Dex and then at the cedar chip valley at his feet.

"Just when we're together," Dex said, and the thought of swearing made Sammy smile again, and Dex smiled, too, then.

"Okay," Sammy said.

"Okay," Dex said. "You first."

"No way," Sammy said. "There's no way I'm going first." He was almost laughing.

And so Dex swore first, a single word. "Ass," he said, and then he leaned back in the swing and kicked emptily at the air.

"Your turn," Dex said.

"Ass," Sammy said.

"You can't say *ass*," Dex said. "I already said ass. You have to pick another swear word."

"Ass bag," Sammy said, and Dex laughed so hard and suddenly that he coughed, and when he finally stopped coughing, he laughed again. "That's not even a swear word, Sammy."

"Well maybe I made it up," Sammy said. "Anyway it's only the first time."

"Shit," Dex said.

"That was going to be my word," Sammy said.

"Why don't you just say *shit bag*," Dex said.

"Fuck," Sammy said, and Dex started coughing again, and they were both laughing.

When the lady with the surgical mask passed on her old bicycle, Dex swore at her so that only Sammy could hear.

"Crazy fucking germ lady," he said.

And soon they were swearing and laughing and swearing and laughing. They swore at dog walkers and cars and pickup trucks and a mailman and at each other, and a woman with blond hair riding past on a Vespa scooter, and when Audrey beeped the horn of the Honda they were laughing so hard that Dex nearly fell off the swing.

In the backseat of the car on the way home they pulled the seat belts across their shoulders and wiped the laughing tears from their eyes. Audrey stretched to see the boys in the rearview mirror. There was a smile in her eyes when she asked them what was so funny, and it seemed to Dex that it was their mother who had picked them up; it was not Audrey after all.

"Nothing," Dex said. "Sammy's just a goofball."

He stuffed himself against the car door then, so that Audrey wouldn't see him, and he mouthed swear words so that only Sammy could see.

Sammy's face was red from laughing. He looked about to explode.

Dex waited until the doors of the Guitar Center closed behind his mother before climbing into the front seat of the car. Their father had two season tickets for White Sox baseball and it was Sammy's turn this year to go to Opening Day, but Dex had made a deal with him. It cost him twenty dollars and shotgun privileges for all of spring break.

Dex had suggested the shotgun clause thinking his mother wouldn't allow Sammy to sit up in the front seat since he was not even ten years old yet, but the plan backfired when Audrey let Sammy sit up there without argument.

The other thing Dex had not considered when they struck the deal was that in their mother's car, whoever sat shotgun also controlled the stereo, and so, through the eighteen-mile drive up Roosevelt Road he had to listen without complaint to "Locomotive Breath," "Thick as a Brick," "Bungle in the Jungle," and the rest of *Jethro Tull's Greatest Hits*. On top of that, he had to suffer through Sammy's abuse of the lyrics to "Aqualung." Sammy looked over the front seat twice to scream-sing the wrong words into the backseat: "And you snatch the raffling lassparettes with deep-sea diver sound."

All Dex could do was plug his fingers into his ears and press his eyes shut.

Still, it wouldn't have been so bad if there hadn't been a White Sox spring training game on the radio. He imagined himself at a summer game with his father—standing at the rail at the bottom of section 153 during batting practice, waiting for foul balls to crack from the wooden bats and into the stands, his father handing him a box of Cracker Jack during the seventh-inning stretch. Like a surprise.

Dex couldn't blame Sammy for his insistence on the wrong words to the song. It was their father who turned Dex on to Jethro Tull first, and then Dex who introduced the band to Sammy. The first time Sammy heard "Aqualung" he had asked Dex to tell him the words to the fast part of the song and Dex told him what he thought they were, and Sammy had a pencil with him and he asked Dex to say the words slowly so he could catch them—he was only six or seven years old then—so Dex said the words slow enough for Sammy to write them down. He said them slowly, like a teacher to a hard-headed child.

"And you *snatch* . . . the *raffling* . . . *lassparettes* . . . with *deep-sea diver* sound," Dex said, as though the words made sense. He even spelled the ridiculous words out for Sammy.

"The *raffling lassparettes?*" Sammy said.

"Yes," Dex said. "The raffling lassparettes."

But Sammy, who was forever asking questions, asked Dex for the definition of a raffling lassparette.

"I don't know," Dex said. "It's a song."

For weeks after, Sammy played "Aqualung." In the house, in the car, in his portable CD player, singing those crazy words until Dex realized how impossible it was that he had got the lyrics right. He finally Googled the song to get the correct words.

At breakfast Dex brought up the lyrics, but he did not look at Sammy while he mentioned the song; he held the box of Honey-Comb cereal in front of his face so it seemed like the discovery wasn't such a big deal.

"I Googled the lyrics to 'Aqualung' this morning," he said.

"You already told me the lyrics," Sammy said.

"Yeah, but I guess I was wrong," Dex said, and he moved the box of Honey-Comb to the side. "What Jethro Tull is actually singing is *and you snatch your rattling last breath.*"

Sammy didn't look up. "Jethro Tull is the name of the *band*," he said. "The singer's name is Ian Anderson."

"Whatever," Dex said. "My point is that there's no such thing as raffling lassparettes."

Sammy clung to the incorrect lyrics, anyway. He sang them loudly in Dex's direction whether "Aqualung" was playing or not, and on the way to the Guitar Center, Sammy hit the replay button three times so he could turn around and champion the snatching of the raffling lassparettes to Dex in the back-seat. There was no escape.

Meanwhile, with every misused word of the song, another pitch was being thrown, another base stolen, another slugger going yard, another second of baseball history was being made without proper witness.

Dex closed his eyes when Sammy hit the replay button a fourth time.

Audrey tapped Sammy on his leg one time and said, "Stop, Sam. Please." She said it so softly Dex was certain Sammy had not heard.

If only Dad were here.

Dex was this close to saying it out loud. Dad would not go for this. If Dad were driving, they would be listening to the White Sox game. That was a fact.

Dex had asked if he could just please stay home and watch the game on TV, but Audrey had dropped her shoulders, had tilted her head and begun to chew on the inside of her cheek, so Dex didn't ask a second time.

When they left home, the White Sox were up 2–0 in the bottom of the second, and the freaky way things seemed to go whenever Dex looked away from the television during baseball games, something amazing or terrible was probably happening.

Still, Dex waited until his mother stopped looking back at him in the car before he turned on the radio. And when the glass doors of the Guitar Center closed and Sammy and Audrey were inside, Dex climbed over the front seat and sat behind the steering wheel. He turned on the radio, switched to the AM dial, and pressed the first memory button to listen to the game.

The announcers had yet to speak. On the radio there was only the throaty and wordless sound of a fan-filled stadium, a kind of roaring filtered through a pillow, but Dex was certain the White Sox were winning. He also felt it was late in the game, the eighth inning maybe, and it was close; it was something about the sound of the fans in the stadium—a worried strain running beneath the slippery hope of a skimpy lead.

They were not ahead by more than one run, Dex thought. He leaned toward the radio and turned his hand palm side up on his knee. He curled his fingers in as if to pull the score and the inning—some greater clue than tone—from the announcers' lips, and when he looked up at the glass wall of the Guitar Center, his mother was pressed against the window looking back at him, her hands framing her face in a visor against the glare.

"Jesus, Audrey," he said.

Dex thought of ducking below the line of the dashboard but he worried his mother would freak out at his disappearance. He raised the volume on the radio. Buehrle had just retired his ninth straight batter. It was 6–5 in the bottom of the eighth. Dex closed his eyes to focus on the game and keep from looking at the Guitar Center, but even then the image of his mother at the window returned to him.

His mother could never pass the dance studio on North Avenue lately without doing the same thing, getting right up against the glass and shading her eyes to stare at the dancers within. On Tuesdays, Dex and Sammy would wait for Audrey to pick them up from the front lobby after her English Department meetings at Francis Parker and they would walk down Clark, and when they got to the dance studio on North Avenue, Audrey would get right up against the plate glass window and shade her eyes. Sometimes Dex would hook his arm through Audrey's to pull her past the studio so she couldn't look, and she would drag her feet, pretending to laugh just to get a peek inside.

"You're obsessed with the dance studio," Dex would say, and Audrey would only shrug and smile and look back to see where Sammy was, and when he walked up to her she would put her arm around his shoulder. Dex was already too tall for her arm around *his* shoulder.

The week before, while Sammy was at a birthday party for one of his classmates, Dex and Audrey walked home without him. Dex ran to the dance studio ahead of her, and to tease her he shaded his eyes at the window just like he knew she would. Audrey laughed, and when she joined him at the window she shaded her eyes with her left hand and put her right arm across his back and rested her hand on his hip.

Inside, there were children standing along two walls watching a boy about Dex's age. He wore black dress pants and a light blue shirt and stood in the middle of the dance floor with his arms held as though he were playing a guitar: his left hand at the invisible neck of the instrument and his right arm around its body, hand suspended in the air, ready to strum the imaginary strings. He stood stiffly, his chest filled with air, and the most serious look on his face, as though he were taking a test for which he had studied a great deal. A woman stood near the boy, instructing the others.

"They're kids," Dex said.

"Yes," Audrey said.

"Is it always kids here?"

"At this time of day," she said, "yes."

A tall girl wearing a black dress walked up to the boy Dex had been watching. Her hair was black and obedient and it brushed her bare shoulders like cloth; she slipped into the space between the boy's arms so that one of his hands held hers and the other settled above her hip. The children watched.

It seemed to Dex as though the boy had not moved the slightest bit to allow the girl into the space he had prepared, but she fit into it with such ease that it seemed as though the boy had accounted for all of her in the phantom hold of his arms. And inside the dance studio no one laughed at the boy and the girl.

At the window, Dex pulled his right hand away from his eyes and shaped it to fit around the lowest ribs of an invisible girl, and it seemed to him that a boy's hands might have been meant for this, for the ribs of a girl.

All the children paired with partners then, and began to dance. And as Dex could not hear any music from the sidewalk, they appeared to him to be dancing in slow motion. The sameness of their steps, their slow swirls around the room, the thin and sweeping gestures of their arms.

Dex mostly watched the serious boy as he danced with his tall partner, held her hand, twirled her away from him and pulled her back into his arms, their eyes locked on each other. There were like little grownups.

He watched Audrey for what felt like minutes as she observed the dancing children. It seemed to him that she was watching the children as though that afternoon might have been her last opportunity to see them dance. As though the world might one day be a place where children would never dance.

It was only when the first blare of a nearby car alarm urged him from his memory that Dex realized he was staring at his mother who was still standing at the glass wall of the Guitar Center, still looking out into the parking lot with her hands in a visor over her eyes. And through the unstopping, bleating complaint of the car alarm Dex did not look away.

He was not certain when he had turned off the radio, nor how long he had been sitting with his hands in the shape of holding a guitar. Neither was he certain what the score of the White Sox game was. Nor if the Sox had won.

But he knew this: he knew he would sit in the passenger seat on the way home. Sammy would complain about the lack of fairness; he would bring up the deal they had struck, and if he had to, Dex would tell Sammy that he would give up shotgun privileges for another week if he just let him have it for this ride back home. Sammy would take that deal. And Dex would sit in the passenger seat on the way home. When his mother pulled out of the parking lot and turned left onto Roosevelt, when she settled into the drive back home and put her hand on his thigh like she did sometimes, Dex would set his hand on top of hers. And if she didn't put her hand on his leg, he would reach for her hand and he would set it there himself. He would set his hand on top of hers then, and he would keep it there. Goddamn it, he would keep it there.

CHAPTER 7

Morning Would Come
(March/April 2008)

After a sunless winter the boys exploded into spring with its promise of summer and its sun, its bicycles and its baseball and pools and sleepovers and summer fests and block parties and Wiffle-ball tournaments in the street.

No one would say that he, Alan, hadn't done the best he could to keep it all together. No one could look him in the eye and say that. For two years he stuck it out, tiptoed around the house putting feelers out for whatever mood Audrey might be in, reacting accordingly, tending to her, mitigating the gloom and the cold in what ways that he could. He waited months for random sweetnesses, a bone now and then. But he was barely in his forties and it was getting more difficult all the time.

He could not keep from comparing the two Audreys—the new and the old. The old Audrey was everything he ever wanted. She was a great mother, she was smart, she was funny, and she was beautiful. There were nights he'd come home to find Audrey had arranged for a babysitter to take Izzy and the boys to a movie for an afternoon. She would come to the door at the sound of his key, wearing some skimpy little number and earrings that dangled, and leaning sultrily against the door frame she'd hike up the hem of her skirt and say something like, *Hey, Mister. Whatcha got in the briefcase?*

Or there was Audrey at the door with a new sundress wearing nothing beneath it, or there she was behind him while he was shaving at the sink, Audrey with her hand in his pajama bottoms on a weekday morning, and all of a sudden she was alive again, lying on the bed after her shower in only her towel, giving herself to him like a new bride. And there he was at the stove again on weekend mornings frying bacon and hash browns and whisking the batter for pancakes, and Audrey standing at the toaster and sipping coffee at the window and smiling, or there he was coming home from work and finding the curtains closed and he was following the scent of a trail of candles, luminaria leading to Audrey lying face down and naked on the bed—hands tucked under her chin in mock sleep—lifting her bottom off the bed in an offering to her husband, to her husband, to her husband.

Even after Khyber, they did their best. They would go to the boys' baseball games together, sit at the top of the aluminum stands and nod hellos to the parents of the other boys. Even after, she might put a hand on his back and make it seem to Alan as though maybe she had returned, as though they still might work it out. Even during those two last years they were together after Khyber, she had rolled over to his side of the bed a couple of times to take Alan inside her. It was enough to make him think that maybe they could do this. Maybe all marriages were like this: men and women muddling through somewhere along the continuum of happiness. You went through rough spots, and if you stuck it out maybe you came through somehow, and maybe the marriage was better for the trouble. Maybe he and Audrey had actually figured it out.

But then it rained. Or it didn't rain. There came a cold day, or a Monday, or a gray day, or a three-day stretch without sun, or the boys had left their dishes in the sink, and it was enough for kisses to go dry and tight, or disappear completely. Or she found some other reason for silence: a glass shattered; a photograph she had forgotten about appeared from a book one of the boys pulled from a shelf, and she wouldn't speak to Alan for a day. And a day became days, and days became weeks.

And just like that she would turn on him again. She could make the winter come in August. She could live a day, a week, a month and never touch him, never even run her fingers across his shoulders as she passed him doing dishes at the sink. Never kiss him. Or if she did, it was perfunctory; her lips tight, dry, muscled.

Or when he touched her in bed she would shift away from him. "Aren't you tired?" she would say, or she would say nothing, inch closer to the wall, and he would feel as though he had made a mistake just to touch her. He would promise himself to never touch her again. How many times had he found himself pulling his fingers away just before touching her?

He couldn't tiptoe around Audrey's moods anymore, wait for her to explode or be sweet or to be normal or to throw him a fucking bone every once in a while. There was still life, wasn't there?

And so, there had been women over the almost four years of their separation. There was Angela, who he'd met in law school. They went out a few times, slept together once, but there was nothing there.

And Molly he met while donating at the police department's annual blood drive. She'd taken his information down before he gave blood, and they got to talking in the ten minutes of filling out forms. Afterward, she'd flipped through the donor files to get his number. They spoke over the phone a couple of times and met for drinks downtown one night, and before she'd finished her second glass of wine she'd leaned across the table and told him she was going to fuck him silly before the night was over. He spent the night at her place and in the morning she woke up and they went at it again. When the phone rang Molly didn't pick it up. She was on top of Alan thrusting her hips at him while her daughter's voice came through the answering machine.

"Are you there, Mommy?" the voice was saying. "I miss you."

Alan turned toward the answering machine and then looked at Molly, who waved it off, gesturing toward her hips like, *I'm busy here*, while her daughter called out to her again.

And there was Renee, whom he'd known long before Audrey, and whom he would never have called were it not for several random appearances she made in his dreams of late.

The dream that finally urged him to call her came in September, the night before the boys' first day of the past school year. They had met, Alan and Renee, while they were undergraduates at Loyola University. They had kissed only once as juniors, but when they met again in graduate school they'd had sex for a summer. She dressed bralessly in boys' T-shirts and roomy pants and wore the tightest underwear imaginable. During one of their nights that summer—near the end of it—Renee had pressed her hips against him, had pulled his hips toward her, and had whispered into his lips that she wished he could stay inside her forever.

In his dream, he had wild and realistic sex with Renee, and even after waking up to go to the bathroom he was able to return to his dream of the braless and steamy Renee. For two weeks he couldn't shake the dream. He sat around the office with random erections and vivid memories of their summer together.

It was October when Alan finally pulled from an old address book a piece of paper with a faded blue-ink phone number Renee had written some twenty years before, and without the slimmest glimmer of confidence that he would ever hear her voice again, he dialed the number.

A recording on the other end informed him that the number he had reached was disconnected, but calls were being taken at another number. When the phone clicked at the other end, Alan heard Renee's voice.

"Hello?" she said.

"Is this Renee?" Alan said.

"Yes, it is," the voice said.

"This is Alan. Alan Taylor."

There was no reason for Alan not to smile through the pause in the line. They'd had a great summer together, and at the very least there would be a phone conversation about the passage of time.

"Oh. My. God," Renee said. "Oh my god."

"Hi," Alan said, and again smiled through the pause that followed.

"I cannot believe this," Renee said.

"And I can't believe I found you through that same old phone number," Alan said.

"Two months ago I might have picked up the phone at that number," she said. "To what do I owe this phone call, Professor Taylor?"

"Not a professor anymore," Alan said. "I left academia and became an attorney."

"Now why in god's name would you ever do such a thing?"

"Long story," Alan said.

"In Chicago still?" Renee said.

"Right here," he said.

"And why the phone call today after a million years?" she said.

Alan untangled the phone cord and looked behind him at his office door.

"A dream," he said.

"A dream made you call me?" she said.

"You appear in dreams of mine, now and then," Alan said, "and I keep telling myself I'll call you. Last week I had another, and so today I finally called."

"What sort of dreams?" Renee said.

"I'm afraid I can't tell you much more about them," Alan said.

She had opened a restaurant, Cricket's, a breakfast place in Bucktown just before the neighborhood had exploded, and had sold it just recently. She had moved out to Racine, Wisconsin, and was opening a restaurant there.

Cricket's. Alan had eaten there. He might have just missed her. Might have been in the same room with her one day.

She doubted that. She would definitely have known if she had been in the same room with him.

She owned a six-room hotel in Mexico, too. "My little hotel," she called it. She was on her way to her little hotel just then, in fact, but would love to talk to him soon and would he promise to call her again?

Alan called her from his office two weeks later, and over an hour-long conversation they covered much of what they had remembered of each other. She had majored in theatre when they first met as undergrads. She had been dating an older guy who was studying to be a dentist.

Mario, as Alan recalled.

Yes, Mario, but she'd agreed to a date with Alan anyway. He remembered Mario.

They had seen the play, *Of Mice and Men*, at the university, and afterward had gone to a cast party on the strength of her friendship with the actors. Alan had made her laugh that night, and when they crossed a street—neither of them could remember the street—he had hooked his arm into hers. She had never felt that before, a guy hooking his arm into hers. She liked his profile, too. And the way his friends greeted him.

How had his friends greeted him?

Like they loved him. Like they were giddy to see him. Like he was the reason they came. It was crowded in the apartment that night and they had danced to a slow song, alone on the floor. Renee had this idea that the floor would fill with the rest of the people at the party, because they were theater people and that's what theater people did at parties, but no one else danced, it seemed.

Later that night they had kissed in a car Alan had borrowed.

Renee remembered that Alan's lips were soft.

"I hope you don't take this wrong, but they reminded me of a woman's lips," Renee said. They were so soft, she was afraid she might bite them.

"Did I ever bite them?" Renee asked.

"Not too hard," Alan said. "But you were dating that Mario guy."

"Yes," Renee said.

"Which sounded like a name for a huge guy," Alan said.

Renee laughed.

Alan had said something that made her laugh.

While they spoke, there was another thing he remembered. They were in a stairwell of one of the older buildings on campus. They had taken a break from Italian class and though it was only afternoon, in the stairwell it was dark in the way he thought a castle might be dark. It was like a small night in the old building and Alan remembered sitting sadly with her—and that when he had left, she had stayed there, elbows on her knees.

Alan wondered if Renee remembered this, but he did not inquire.

When they met again, Alan was in grad school and Renee was waiting tables at an off-campus grill and was not dating Mario. They went to the zoo. He remembered holding hands with her. She remembered what she was wearing that day. She was wearing men's jeans and a white blouse with a tank top beneath. Back at his apartment he kissed her for only the second time in four years.

"'I want to be inside you,' is what you told me," Renee said.

"And I remember the underwear you had on that afternoon," Alan said. "They were as yellow as the sun, and impossibly tight."

"I still like them tight," Renee said, and Alan checked the office door.

During the lull that followed, Renee asked if he had married.

Alan said that he had. He told her of Audrey and what life had become for them. They had separated and were making the best of it. So far as they knew how. Alan told Renee of Dex and Sammy and how there was never a space between one sport and the next. He did not tell her of Isabel.

Renee had nearly married as well.

They began to speak on Tuesdays. Alan would call her after his meetings with the mayor, and once, while she was away at her little hotel in Mexico, Renee called and left a message for him on his office line.

In early October, Renee surprised Alan with a visit to one of Dex's floor hockey games at the park district. Alan hadn't seen her in nearly twenty years but when he saw her leaning against the wall inside the gymnasium doors he was almost certain it was Renee. She tilted her head toward the floor and watched the boys play through the curls that tumbled into her eyes. Alan sat at the high end of the bleacher seats not twenty yards away. Twice, when she caught Alan's eyes, she shook her hair from her face and smiled, then turned back to the boys on the court.

Alan wondered if Audrey, who was sitting in a folding chair next to him, could see the pounding thump of his heart through his autumn jacket.

Renee called him after work the next day. Her first words on the phone were these:

"He looks just like you."

"I thought that was you," Alan said. "You look good, Renee."

"I hope you don't think I was stalking you," she said. "I had plans with a couple of girlfriends in Chicago last night and figured I'd catch a couple of innings of Dex's hockey game."

"Periods," Alan said. "Innings in baseball, periods in hockey."

"Whatever," Renee said, and Alan laughed.

"He's a good-looking kid," Renee said.

"You just said that I was good looking," Alan said.

"No, I didn't," Renee said.

"Yes, you did," Alan said. "First you said he looked just like me and then you said he was good looking."

"Damn," Renee said. "I guess I did."

After that phone call Alan thumbed through a stack of papers and submitted a proposal to attend a convention for city attorneys in San Francisco that spring. There was no reason why it would not be approved, he thought, and when it was he would ask Renee to join him for a weekend there. She owned a restaurant and a hotel. She could get off work if she wanted to.

It was approved in November, but Alan waited until January to ask Renee. Between those dates there were nearly a dozen Tuesdays of phone calls.

When he heard the phone click from its cradle at the other end the next Tuesday, when he heard the word *hello*, what Alan said was this:

"Hey. Do you like San Francisco?"

Not the line he had planned to begin their conversation. He hadn't thought that far ahead. At work that day, he had spent so much time wondering how to bring up the attorney's conference April, that he hadn't considered an opening line.

But when the question was out, when it hovered in the immense configuration of telephone wires and boxes and poles between them, for the second or two of silence it took for Renee to place his voice, recall his face, consider a response, Alan was glad it was out there.

As a matter of fact, she loved San Francisco. She'd been there many times. Had lived there for a weird six months, in fact, and was there a reason he asked?

There was.

And would he like to share that reason?

He would be happy to share it. He would be going to San Francisco in early April, to attend the National Convention for City Attorneys.

She laughed. She didn't think a more exciting reason for visiting San Francisco could ever be had. She had never contemplated that line of work, but now that she'd been informed of giant gatherings of such people she wondered if it wasn't yet too late to consider the career herself.

Well, he was afraid it was much too late to jump on that bandwagon.

Did *he* like San Francisco?

He'd never been, though the way people spoke of it, it seemed it was a place he could live and be happy.

It was a great place to live, she agreed. But she could never *work* there.

What did she mean?

When she lived in San Francisco for those six months, she had to work. And there was something about the place that made it hard to work. She wanted to wake up every morning thinking, *What should I do today?* Yes, now that she thought about it, maybe it wasn't so much a place to live. What she meant was that it was an excellent place to visit. Anyway, there were places he should not neglect if he could only tear himself away from the other city attorneys.

While she spoke, Alan imagined Renee smoking a cigarette on the edge of a hotel bed that looked over the bay, where (she was telling him now) seals barked and knocked each other off piers in the late morning.

Seals at play, Alan thought. He had spent a summer observing seals at play as an undergraduate. People could watch that for hours. Pinnipeds clamoring for desirable purchase in the sun.

Sometimes, Renee was saying, they popped up out of nowhere and scared the shit out of kayakers cruising the bay.

He could not recall ever seeing Renee smoke—did not think that one could even smoke in hotels anymore—

but just the same, he imagined her sitting on the edge of the bed, wearing skintight underwear and perhaps a dress shirt of his—maybe even a tie—a rill of smoke rising from her cigarette, wavering as it dissipated toward the ceiling.

He asked if she would like to meet him out there, and for the splittest of seconds the line went quiet. And so as not to extend that silence, Alan quickly spoke to fill it. There were only two workshops he would have to attend and they would not neglect any of those things in San Francisco that should not be neglected. They could go to Chinatown and Haight-Ashbury, sit in coffee shops in Berkeley Square, and do whatever it was that people did out there, they could laugh at the seals, or even take data on them—he could show her how to do that—but if she couldn't get off work that weekend he would understand.

"I'm the boss of everything I do," she said.

"What?"

"I'm the boss of everything I do," she said again. "I can get off work whenever I want."

She would have to look into a couple of things, but she could use a break. She would see if her friend Jane could manage things that weekend. Anyway, she was off to her yoga class now and would it be all right if she called him back in a day or two?

It would be all right.

It was seven days later when the call came to him at his desk at the Daley Center. He picked up the phone and Renee said, "Did you mean what you said about San Francisco?" And Alan felt his heart pound in his chest.

"Of course I meant it," Alan said. "Are you considering my invitation?"

"I already cleared it with my boss."

"She seems like a great boss," he said.

"Oh, she's wonderful," she said. "And quite sexy."

"No doubt," Alan said.

"At which hotel are you booked?" Renee said.

"The Prospect."

"Ooh la la," Renee said.

"It's just that there'll be hundreds of city attorneys at the Westin, where the conference is, and they're mostly uninteresting."

"Should I get my own room?" Renee said.

"You should not," Alan said. "If you're okay with it, you can stay with me."

"Are you okay with it?" she said.

"I'm good," he said, and he fiddled with the twisted phone cord and checked to see that his office door was closed.

After that phone call, Alan called Audrey and told her to mark those dates, the fourth through the sixth of April, on her calendar. He had been asked to represent the police department at a convention for city attorneys.

"It should be fine," Audrey said. That was the week after the boys' spring break. Hers as well. She had been thinking, by the way, about spending a few days of her break in Iowa if it was okay with Alan. Her mother was not doing well, she said. And her father's mental health had taken a turn, too.

Alan told her that would be fine. He would take some vacation time to spend with the boys.

"I'd leave on that Saturday morning, the twenty-ninth of March."

"It's fine," Alan said.

"I'd be back in time for the convention," she promised. "April first. No later than the second. I'll be back in time."

"It's fine," Alan said again. "Definitely. Go."

They had been trying, Audrey and Alan, to do something together with Dex and Sammy every other weekend. They had gone ice-skating at Ridgeland Commons a few times and had a number of Scrabble and Monopoly marathons. And they had two all-day pizza-making tournaments at Alan's place, too: one in January and one in early March. Twice, though, Audrey came to Alan's apartment alone and unannounced.

The first time she came to his place, he opened the door to find her tapping on it with a bottle of white wine in one hand and wineglasses tinkling in the other.

"Hey, take these and wait right here," she said. "There's more stuff in the Mazda," and she ran like a schoolgirl back to the car in a skirt and sweater that she seemed to fill like a brand new girlfriend. Whiffs of her perfume hovered in the cold humidity of the doorway, and while he watched her running to her car like a girl he could smell the old Audrey, and when she returned she had a roasting pan filled with Mediterranean Chicken with garlic and rosemary, capers and new potatoes, and there was the old sweetness. She could reveal it whenever she wanted, it seemed.

If she had called him ahead of time he would have told her that he had a ton of work to do for the department, that it was not a good day. But she had not called him ahead of time, and she had put some effort into the meal. He could see that. And it had been a long time. It had been a long time.

That first time she came over it was December, and after they ate, they watched TV for a while. Alan sat on the floor because although he didn't know exactly what Audrey was up to, he hated that she could turn things around whenever she wanted. He hated that she could just come over in her little skirts and sundresses with wine and kiss him full on the lips and have whatever the hell she wanted. And he didn't want it to be so easy for her. So he sat on the floor to watch television so she couldn't curl up next to him so easily, so she couldn't just stretch out on his lap and reach back with her arms so that her breasts could be right there for him to touch so easily.

But there she was, doing her nightly stretches, and there she was yawning and winding down, and there she was nudging his legs so she could rest her head on his chest, and there she was reaching back with her arms to scratch at the back of his neck. There she was.

And the thing was that by the time Audrey spent that night, Alan knew that it meant nothing. He knew that if he attached any value to her visit—if he thought it meant she had turned a corner somehow—it would only be a week or two before the real truth was revealed. That she just wanted to get laid. Pure and fucking simple.

When Audrey left in the morning, Alan took a shower. He soaped himself generously, scrubbed her away. There was a deep gloom about Audrey, a wishlessness he could no longer be part of.

And by then he'd been talking to Renee for two months. By then he'd begun to think of this thing with Renee as a strange kind of courtship. He'd begun to think of Renee as a very real possibility, and strangely enough, the night with Audrey felt like an infidelity to Renee. He had talked with Renee about Audrey often enough, and he had told Renee that it was over with Audrey. All of a sudden there was a secret he had to keep from Renee.

The second time Audrey came by unannounced it was on a Saturday night in February. Alan was reading on the living room couch with a clip light attached to his book. Audrey knocked on the door and waited, knocked and waited again, and then talked softly to Alan through the door.

"I know you're in there, Alan," she said. "Your car's out front."

Inside, Alan wondered what Audrey was wearing.

"Alan?"

"It's me, Audrey. Come open the door. I've got something for you out here, Alan."

Alan deliberated over every inch of his movement into the kitchen, testing the floor for creaks with small-weighted, measured steps. Still, though, he could hear her from the kitchen.

Renee asked Alan each week if the San Francisco trip was still on, and each week Alan said absolutely. It was still on.

Alan had a week of baseball planned with the boys—*preseason* he called it. He rented out the batting cages at Stella's for the boys on three afternoons and invited their friends from school. They rented a gym at the local middle school for fielding practice. They made pizzas and watched two spring training games on television. They planned to watch a different baseball movie every night, but after watching *The Sandlot* on the first night, they decided to watch it every night.

Alan had the boys call Audrey at their grandparents' house in Iowa before they went to bed each night. She never asked to speak to Alan, which was fine. Her emails were enough. The first message warned of *all hell breaking loose* in Iowa, and in the second email Audrey warned that what had begun as a five-day visit looked like it was turning into double that, and so Alan made arrangements for Ed and Sandy, across the street, to take care of the boys until his return from San Francisco.

The third email seemed to be a detailed account of every minute of Audrey's day. He skimmed it as it scrolled upward on his BlackBerry screen while the boys were taking bunts in the batting cages. Every day, it seemed, the emails came in lengthy ramblings across his BlackBerry. He shook his head and mumbled the page numbers as they passed his screen.

Alan dropped the boys off at Ed and Sandy's on Thursday night, and when he returned to the house his cell phone rang. The caller said nothing in the second of silence that followed Alan's greeting, but he knew it was Renee. Something in the silence.

"Are you sure about this?" Renee said.

"I'm sure," he said.

"I can still book my own room."

"Don't," he said.

She would take a cab from the airport and call Alan on his cell phone when she reached the lobby of the Prospect Hotel.

On the airplane on Friday morning, Alan's breathing was labored. He yawned incessantly; for oxygen, he told himself, his eyes tearing up with every yawn. He checked his planner. Renee's cell phone number was on a Post-it attached to the date. He shut the planner and opened the *Sun-Times*. He flipped past the city news section for the third time. The horoscopes. He yawned. He wiped his eyes. A surge of something pumped through his veins to his heart. Adrenaline it felt like. Or anger.

Deep breath. Slow release. Corrections. Diaphragmatic. Cardiac. Corrections.

He opened his planner again and looked at the conference schedule. Continental breakfast eight to nine, symposium at nine fifteen, presentation at ten thirty. He would slip out before lunch and meet up with Renee.

Another surge. Renee? Was that it? Yes. It was San Francisco, a conference he would learn nothing from, a hotel room with Renee. And there, at the bottom of the box for Saturday, April 5, was one more thing. It was opening day for Little League baseball. He would miss Dex's double-header, and Sammy's first game. It was Renee, it was Dex, it was Sammy, it was everything.

It was Audrey, bottom line. She, the source of the anger. She, the stilted breath.

"I could have stayed with her forever," he said of his wife. Aloud he had said it.

Had she been there—not just physically, but been there to hold, a wife who touched him now and then—had there been *that* he never would have called Renee, never would have looked her up in the first place. Never asked her to San Francisco. It was too late now.

Eight fifty Chicago time. Sandy would have just returned from dropping the boys off at school. Audrey in Iowa, sleeping still. Like her heart. In a kind of sleep as well. On the phone the night before she had told him to be safe on his trip. *Be careful*, she had said. Always sweeter on the phone. It used to be enough to fool him sometimes, to make him think she'd be glad to see him walking through the door. But she couldn't pull off that sweetness in person. He always came home to something different.

She was a different person than the Audrey he had met after Renee. Even her *name* was different. When he first saw the name *Audreanna* written on her driver's license, he said nothing. He rolled the name around his tongue and teeth for a while, like a song, until it became a word for his wife.

Weeks later, on the morning that followed their first night of love, Alan gave Audrey a birthday card on which he'd written her given name, Audreanna, and she had come close to crying.

She had been called Audreanna as a child, she told him, and she had loved her name at first, but started going by Audrey when she entered middle school.

And while Alan made love to her again on that birthday afternoon—when he whispered her given name into her neck and into her eyes, when he kissed her given name into her ears and her lips and her hair—she had trembled and cried, had shuddered with him inside her, with her given name touching her everywhere.

And long afterward, mostly in moments of sweetness, he began to call her Audreanna. Sometimes he would call her *Sweet Audreanna*.

Then came the night of Khyber Pass. Then came the deep fog of her gloom. Those three days in June when she didn't say a word to Sammy or Dex or Alan. Sammy was only six years old then—the summer before he started first grade.

Only once more in those years of sadness that followed did Alan called her Sweet Audreanna. It slipped out somehow. Perhaps she had urged it on with some flicker of sweetness, or he had mistaken her sadness for something else.

"Good night, Sweet Audreanna," he had said.

They were in bed and Audrey had a book open at her hips. She put her finger to a sentence to hold her place and looked at Alan over the reading glasses she had dipped on her nose.

"Enough," she said. "Enough with the Audreanna."

Later that night, in the dark of their bedroom, she rolled toward the wall and said, "I can't do this, Alan. I can't do this anymore."

"What does that mean, Audrey?" he had asked her. "What the fuck does that mean?" But she said nothing.

It was the last time he had called her Sweet Audreanna. They could have had a fucking marriage. Hadn't that been the plan? A marriage? A family? Maybe this was cheating, what he was about to do, but she had cheated him as well. A kind of cheating it was. She had cheated him of life since that night. Four years. She'd cheated Sammy and Dex as well. He was done with the wasting of life. It was a brand new day.

In the taxicab, the sun was like a hot hand on the side of his face. Warm. Wrong, it seemed. Sun in April.

Alan was jolted from sleep when the taxicab stopped in front of the Prospect Hotel. He had only fifteen minutes to spare before the first workshop, so he shouldered his bags and walked the three blocks to the conference center.

In the auditorium, he thumbed through his folder and filled out the workshop evaluation form before the presentation had begun, and throughout the lecture he fought against the distractions spinning in his head. At eleven forty-five he was walking toward the Prospect. The April sun was the sun of Chicago in June.

He had packed lightly—a shoulder bag and backpack—but a bead of sweat trailed from his underarm into the sleeve of his T-shirt. If he talked to Audrey tonight he thought this was a thing he would tell her. He would tell her it was April and he was walking outside and sweating. Renee would be in the bed next to him. Through the phone Audrey would sound sweet.

Alan's BlackBerry vibrated and rang. Loudly, it seemed, in this new place. It startled him. He did not answer it, though—he pressed a button to stop the ringing—for there was Renee across the street, a cell phone in her ear, looking up at the hotel as though she expected Alan to be at the window of his room waiting for her to appear on the sidewalk below. One suitcase. Blue jeans. White T-shirt. Bra.

Did she remember that night in graduate school when they drank margaritas at La Fiesta on Wrightwood and Halsted? In the car on the way home. Did she remember Alan saying he didn't think he could ever love her? Did she remember getting out of the car at the stop sign and walking away without argument?

Great hair she still had. The way she let it fall in her eyes. Looked at the world through it. As though she were offering herself to the world on one condition: that it first looked at her hair.

What was she? Forty-four? No. Forty-five. Same as he. Breasts like a super-heroine.

Alan came upon her from behind. He set his bags down and pressed his fingers into her hips to surprise her, and she turned about so suddenly that for an instant he worried he had touched the hips of a stranger. She wrapped her arms around him quickly and firmly and Alan dropped his phone, laughing only when Renee's arms were so tight around his waist that she had become a certainty. She pressed her hips against him then, and kissed him completely. For the length of a kiss his lips were lost in the warmth and fullness of hers. They were not Audrey's lips.

When Alan felt himself harden against her, he pulled away, but Renee pulled his hips to hers and pressed against him. She took her mouth from his, tugging at his lower lip as she pulled away.

"I just called you," she said.

"I know. I wanted to surprise you."

"You did," she said.

"Yes, I surprised you so much I dropped my phone," he said, and he pulled away from her to pick up his phone.

After they checked in, Renee threaded her arm through the crook of his and they waited for the elevator.

"You're still thin," she said. "And not a single gray hair."

"I have six, actually," he said. "You just can't see them."

The elevator arrived and Alan pressed sixteen. He leaned against the gilded and mirrored wall opposite Renee, who stared and smiled and closed her teeth on her bottom lip. When the door opened, two men were waiting for the elevator.

"Going down?" the first man said, and he walked in before Alan and Renee left the tiny room.

The second man never moved. He stared at Renee's breasts.

"Oh, my," he said.

In the hallway, as he walked slightly behind Renee to get to room 1610, Alan said, "Did you hear what that guy said?"

Renee shifted her steps so that they matched Alan's. She returned her arm to his waist. She was smiling.

"No, what?" Renee said.

"He said, 'Oh, my,'" Alan said. "He looked at your breasts and he said, 'Oh, my.'"

Renee laughed. Tiny shakes of her head. Her hair bounced in loose twists of life. It was alive.

"Do people really say such things?" he said.

"Not *people*," Renee said. "*Men*. Men say such things."

Alan shrugged as if to apologize for men.

Inside the hotel room, Renee dropped her bag in the shadowy dark and hugged Alan as though she'd been waiting forever to hold him. Her hands locked at the nape of his neck. Another kiss. And then Renee was staring at him.

If he could just brush his teeth and splash water on his face, he'd be ready to hit the streets in minutes. He was starving.

"Me first," she said. She had to pee.

Alan sat on the bed in the dark while Renee's sounds—trebled and tinny—were transported through the inches she'd left open between the door and its frame. This is my body, Renee was saying. These are my sounds. They located him in time, and for a moment nothing temporal seemed to exist between that moment and the day he had last been alone with her.

Alan walked to the window where two halves of wine-dark curtains met. He whipped them open and a sudden shock of sun exploded into the room. He shut them just as quickly and sat at the edge of the bed.

When Renee emerged from the bathroom she was wearing a baby blue T-shirt pulled tight across her chest.

"Oh, my," Alan said.

Renee laughed, and in minutes they were outside, where the exploding sun belonged.

They had cups of soup and shared a corned beef sandwich at a deli, and immediately they began to realize their telephoned imaginings of a day in San Francisco: sipping espresso at an outdoor café, walking down the crookedest street in the world, riding cable cars. Renee bought bath salts from a scented store and when they passed reggae musicians, she pulled the salts from her purse and rattled them like maracas, shook them while she danced in the street. They watched the barking seals play.

On the deck of a restaurant boat they drank daiquiris out of plastic cups and laughed.

They selected tourists and chose secrets for them.

Alan pointed to a short-haired blonde wearing running shoes and a dress. "When she was fourteen, she had a black lover on a family vacation. That skinny guy over there," Alan said, "saves his convention nametags in a shoebox."

Renee thought that was weird of him to say. Did he save his as well?

"Maybe," Alan said.

"That woman there, in the straw hat," Renee said. "She's skipping the workshops for City Attorneys tomorrow afternoon to lie naked on her hotel bed."

Alan laughed.

"Just kidding," she said. "That's what I like to do."

Renee leaned into Alan's ear. She touched his neck, her fingers cold with daiquiri sweat, and whispered nothing, but looked at him then as though she had promised him sex.

They walked.

In an art store Alan bought an old framed photograph of Lou Gehrig and Joe DiMaggio for Dex, and one of Jackie Robinson for Sammy.

Renee asked what Dex was like.

What did she mean?

"You know, what is he like?"

He was something else, Alan said. Great kid. Nuts about baseball, good speller, roots for the underdog in every sport.

"Tell me a story about him," she said.

"A story," Alan said, and they sat on a bench outside the store.

"When Dex was five," Alan began, "we were driving home from having a catch in the park one day. It was a warm, late winter afternoon and about a block away from home he started crying and I asked him what was wrong.

"'It's just so nice outside,' he said.

"'Does that make you sad?' I asked him.

"'No,' he said.

"'Then why are you sad?' I asked him.

"'Because the summer is going to end,' he said.

"It wasn't even spring yet," Alan told Renee.

They were kitty-corner from a candy store, and Renee kissed Alan.

"And what about Sammy?" Renee said.

"Sammy," Alan said. "Baseball is life for Sammy."

They started walking again.

"Guitar, too," Alan said. "He plays the guitar pretty well, too."

"Tell me a story about Sammy," Renee said.

"We started collecting baseball cards when he was three years old, and he used to shuffle his like playing cards and throw them all around, but my cards I kept in boxes and after—on the night Audrey and I separated, I was on my way out the door and I had Sammy in my arms and he looked down at Dex and then he turned back to me and he whispered this in my ear," and Alan leaned into Renee's ear to whisper what Sammy said to him: "Does this mean I can have your baseball cards?"

"You're a good father, Alan," she said, and she kissed him again.

"Let's walk," he said.

They walked.

Renee's feet grew sore.

Should they start heading back to the hotel?

They should.

Should they shower at the hotel and then find a place to eat?

They should.

Renee held his arm while they walked. Twice she seemed to go for his hand but touched his wrist, slid her arm into his instead, and the early evening settled on San Francisco.

They passed shops that began to look familiar even to Alan, each adding its aroma to the night. There was dark chocolate and cinnamon and coffee, leather, new shoes, and wood; there was pasta in steaming water, there was shrimp, garlic, and rosemary. There was bread. There was the smell of a thousand fishes swimming in the bay, and a thousand more sizzling in skillets.

At a corner of Fisherman's Wharf, Renee hooked her finger into Alan's belt loop and pulled him into a boutique. In the back of the store, a winding iron staircase led to a railed loft. Alan touched Renee's waist and pointed to the higher ground. He'd be up there when she was done touching everything in the store.

On the upper level, sundressed mannequins posed on a bench looking out over the ground floor. They sat sexily, slenderly, elbows on their knees so that a man could look down their sundresses at their stiff-nippled breasts.

Alan looked for Renee on the lower level. There. She held a tiny tank top—a shirt for an infant, it seemed—at her chest. She tilted her head in a mirror, pretended she didn't know Alan was watching. She looked up at Alan and raised her eyebrows at him.

Alan gave her the thumbs up and Renee winked.

He walked among a maze of sundresses. There was room to spare on these racks. The easy swish of metal on metal like this. Drapes in the hotel, too. Easy swish.

There were words on some of these dresses. Cursive.

Il vestito.

Italian. The dress.

Il vestito di Maria. Il vestito di Lina.

Names of women.

Il vestito di Lorelei. Il vestito di Rosalie.

Lorelei. That Styx song, Alan thought, and when he held the hanger of the next dress in his hand he stopped flipping through the rack. It was a white sundress printed with a splash of big flowers in blues and greens and yellows running down the sides. It seemed to drop its petals everywhere. Written in cursive across the front of the dress was his wife's name, Audreanna.

Il vestito di Audreanna.

The dress of Audreanna.

Of all the names for a sundress.

What size? Four. Would it fit Audrey?

Il vestito di Audreanna.

Alan flinched at the touch of fingernails on his back.

"Would you like me to try that on for you?" Renee said. "We can both fit into the dressing room up here, if you'd like."

"You scared me," he said.

She kissed his neck. Breasts against his shoulder blades.

Alan quick-laughed through his nose and returned the dress to the rack.

"You ready?" he said.

Yes. Her feet were killing her.

Alan smiled, but as they began to walk, Audreanna's sundress returned to him. He should have bought it. Could it be altered to fit her? In a lifetime, would he ever find another sundress named Audreanna? Would she hate or love such a dress?

Was there something wrong? Renee wondered.

Alan yawned. Wiped his eye.

Just a little tired. How far were they from the hotel?

Twenty minutes, she guessed. If she remembered correctly there was a little bit of a restaurant tucked between two houses up ahead. Shrimp and pasta place. Would that be all right?

It would.

Was he sure there was nothing wrong?

He was sure. He was fine. A little tired.

The restaurant, an accomplice in the conspiracy of San Francisco, was a thing Audrey would love. It was enough to wake a person up, to slap a woman out of whatever sleep into which she might have fallen. The place was a pilferer of hearts.

They drank wine and ate bruschetta. Renee closed her eyes with each bite and wished aloud for the appetizer never to end.

Did he like it?

The best he'd ever had.

No, really.

Really. It was that good.

She did not ask him again what was bothering him.

Was she ready to head back to the hotel, and would she mind, when they reached it, if he showered first?

Alan closed the door while he took his shower. I am showering in a hotel room, he thought. Renee, my girlfriend from college, who loves being naked in hotels, is mere feet away.

I am married to Audrey. Audreanna.

The easy swish of the shower curtain. The steamed mirror. Mirrors everywhere in hotels. What was that trick? Blow-dry the steam away. Renee in the next room. Clothes in his bag outside the door.

He left the bathroom wearing pajama bottoms and a T-shirt. Renee was sitting against the headboard wearing a hotel towel, knees pulled to her chest.

"Your turn," he said.

"In a bit," she said. "First things first." She held her hands up and scratched her fingers at the air between them. "I thought I might scratch your back for a minute."

Renee pulled the covers down and patted the space next to her.

Alan lay down and wrapped his arms around a pillow. He turned his head toward the wall. She lifted his T-shirt from his waist and pulled it toward his neck until he shifted his arms and head in agreement with its removal.

On his back, Renee's fingernails were charged and certain. Hard and smooth and red. She dragged them from his tailbone and across his back to his neck. His scalp.

Jesus, she was a comb with ten fingers, her nails slow-dragging through his hair. The charge of it in his abdomen. How long since a woman's fingers had been in his hair?

I could have stayed with you forever, Audrey.

Now. Fingers. Ten of them. Collected at their tips—rolled like ball bearings—tingled at his sides and in the hollows of his arms. The charge of them.

She was straddling him now, sitting on his backside. Fingernails rolling over his back. Her towel fell from her body and onto the back of his legs. He felt her pull it away and heard it fall to the floor. He felt the weight of her lift, felt her fingers flatten on his back and trail to his neck. When she bent over to put her lips into his ear, a breast whispered against his back, the weight of it like a finger.

She was going to take a shower. He shouldn't go anywhere. And she walked into the bathroom.

Jesus. What the fuck was he doing?

He had a family. Sons. A wife.

Hard.

Damn. He had not called the boys at Ed and Sandy's. He had wished them good luck at their games this weekend and said he would call them tonight. He would apologize in the morning. It was a crazy night, he would tell them both. That would not be a lie.

Water running. Renee taking a shower. Alan was shirtless. He adjusted himself upward. Hard still. Beginning to soften.

What time was it? Nine thirty. Renee would come out of that bathroom in minutes, in all of her naked glory. Then what?

What was different now from the thoughts that had tumbled through his head when he invited her to San Francisco a month before? Nothing had changed in his marriage. Audrey had not changed for the better, had not become again the wife he thought he had married sixteen years before: the one who smiled, who touched, who kissed like she meant it. The one who surprised him with a candlelit bathroom when he came home late from work on an evening in the spring. The one who asked him to sit back on the bed and relax while she modeled shirts she'd just bought for him. The one who'd made him *feel*. What was different now?

Renee. No less beautiful than she'd been in college. She was funny and sexy and pretty and smart. No muscles in her lips. Taking a shower now. He could get up from the bed, open the door—certain it was unlocked—swish the shower curtain open and take Renee into his arms. She wouldn't hesitate to take him into her hands, her mouth, her everywhere, right then. Why was he sorry he'd invited her to San Francisco?

Fuck. He should just take off his bottoms and lie on his back. Pull the fucking trigger. Audrey wouldn't even care, would she? They didn't even have a marriage.

He would lie there with his fingers locked under his head and wait for Renee to return, allow her to do with him what she would, take him into any part of her she wanted. She used to look at him for hours. She would touch herself in front of him. This is my body. Watch me.

Wasn't that why he had asked her to come in the first place?

The water in the bathroom stopped.

Or he could feign sleep.

The water dripped to a stop.

He could feign sleep. He had told her he was tired. The swish of the shower curtain.

She would believe him. He'd had a long day. He would breathe deeply and heavily when she came to bed.

What if she reached for him? Slipped her hands under and took hold of him in her fingers? Held him. He would harden. That was certain. Could he *will* away an erection? What engorged man could feign flaccidity?

The door opening. Soft steps. Tiptoed steps. The click of the light on the stand, and then darkness; the bed shifting with the weight of a woman. Fingernails again. Wide circles spiraling into a tight circle. Scratching in the shape of something else now. A heart. Small hearts now. Small hearts inside bigger hearts.

Closer. Her leg over his. Her breast at his shoulder. Not Audrey's breast. Her hand flat on his lower back now, slipping into his pajamas, smoothing across his backside. Smart to have adjusted himself upward while she showered. Harder to take hold of him, to discover the thing a man could not pretend.

Breathe. The depth, the length of sleep.

Her lips on his shoulder.

Breathe. Careful. The betrayal of a moan.

Her finger tracing the split of his buttocks. What had Leopold Bloom called it in *Ulysses*? Mesial groove? Medial? The statue of a nude in the park. Leo. Medial.

Breathe. Breathe.

Fuck. What was he doing? Renee's fingernails on his ass. A woman who knew nothing about him. With whom he shared little more than sex nearly twenty years before. She knew nothing about him. She knew one story about Dex, one story about Sammy. And she only knew this because Alan had betrayed them.

She did not even know Alan had a daughter.

He had not told her about Isabel.

Renee's fingernails trailing his legs now.

He had betrayed them all. Was betraying them right now. Dex and Sammy back home. He could have been back there with them now, tucking them in the night before their first baseball games of the season. Getting ready to celebrate their first wins or comfort them through their first losses. And Audrey was in Iowa dealing with death and Alzheimer's. Jesus. He had betrayed her, too. She had not yet come to grips with Isabel's death and now this.

Renee. Pulling his pajama pants past the curve of his ass now. Pressing her breasts against his ass.

And Isabel. He had betrayed Isabel, as well. Betraying her now. Betraying her most of all. Sweet Isabel. The one person from whom he could no longer keep secrets. She could see him now. Sweet Isabel who had fallen in love with Daisy Buchanan and Nick Carraway and the word *couscous* on the night she disappeared into a world darker than any F. Scott Fitzgerald could ever have dreamed. Sweet Isabel who held the possibility of one more kiss out to him that night at Khyber Pass.

If you want to kiss me any time during the evening, just let me know, she had said. They had become for him—though it could not have been true—Isabel's last words. The possibility of that kiss hovering out there like a ghost for five years now.

Renee's fingers slowed to a stop. Was she beginning to wonder whether he was sleeping? Was she thinking of reaching beneath him to take hold of him? No man could sleep through that kind of touching.

Breathe. Breathe.

She pulled Alan's pajamas back up. The weight of her shifting in the bed. Did she turn to the wall? Was she facing the curtains?

The tick of her watch on the stand.

Would she go to sleep?

The sound of his blinking eyelids.

Did she hear these things?

What would tomorrow hold for Renee? For him? For them? He would worry of tomorrow then. He would worry of tomorrow, if.

Breathe. Sleep will come. Sleep will come. Sleep will come.

And sleep did come. Shifting, twisting, tumbling with dreams, sleep came. And in the still-dark of morning—when the full weight of a woman lifted from the bed and dressed in the sliver of yellow light from a bathroom; unchained the door, opened it, closed it again, and slipped away without a backward glance—sleep, for Alan, would end.

He would lie awake in bed, alone, heavy with the first remembering of an almost-affair. The day. The night. Renee pressing against him in front of the Prospect, the promise of sex she'd whispered in his ear, her fingers on his back, her breasts against him, her smell, bath salts, her lips. Her leaving. All his to remember now.

Alan sat against the headboard and there he imagined Renee walking down the hallway, at the elevator, in the lobby, walking away from the Prospect.

It would be Saturday soon. It was Saturday now. When he was certain that Renee had entered a cab to begin her return to her world, he would walk to the window and open the curtains to the gray-black morning and look outside.

And when daylight came, he would call United and move his flight up to Saturday evening. He would call Sandy between the morning workshops to check on the boys. He would leave a message for her to call his hotel when they returned from the ball field.

In the afternoon, he would return to that boutique. He would climb the stairs for Audreanna's sundress. He would have them fold it and set it on a cloud of tissue and place it in a box. He would buy gift paper and ribbon and wrap the sundress and he would hold it on his lap on the airplane. He would take the sundress home to Audrey. Where it belonged.

But now it was still dark, and so he would return to bed. And there he would wait for the earth to roll, to roll, to roll toward the light.

CHAPTER 8

A List of the Dead
(March/April 2008)

From: Audrey Taylor <ataylor@ameritech.net>
To: Alan Taylor <alantaylor@comcast.net>
Date: Sat, 29 Mar 2008 13:15:09 +0000

Alan,

I've probably got ten minutes or so to write before getting back home. God forbid Dad wakes up from his nap and finds he's alone. I'm at Mercy Hospital in Burlington, writing this from a computer for patients' families. I wasn't at the house for a minute before she practically tackled me at the door and told me to take her to the hospital. They want to keep an eye on her through the weekend, run tests, etc. She's in worse shape than I thought.

   I know I promised I'd be back well before you left for San Francisco, but it looks like I won't be able to fly out of here until Friday at least. Will you be able to see that the boys get to school on Friday? Ed and Sandy will help out, I'm sure. I'm sure I'll be back by Saturday. God help me if I'm stuck here past then. I'll check my email from the house or from here, tomorrow, so let me know if you get this.

I've been in Iowa for an hour. It feels like I've been here all week. It feels like what you feel just before all hell breaks loose.

From: Audrey Taylor <ataylor@ameritech.net>
To: Alan Taylor <alantaylor@comcast.net>
Date: Sun, 30 Mar 2008 18:08:03 +0000

Alan. I'm going to be here for ten more days. I haven't the strength right now to tell you the long story. Please, please, please talk to Ed and Sandy to see if they can handle the boys while you're in San Francisco. Tell them I'll make it up to them.

From: Audrey Taylor <ataylor@ameritech.net>
To: Alan Taylor <alantaylor@comcast.net>
Date: Mon, 31 Mar 2008 22:59:23 +0000

Hi, Alan.
Sorry about my hasty email yesterday. Jesus. I was going to ask Sammy to hand you the phone when the boys called last night, but I couldn't bear to rehash the day. Dex said the boys are set to stay at Ed and Sandy's while you're in San Francisco. Sorry about this, Alan.

I promised the details of the long story. Here goes.

Can you believe Mom had this all set up with the hospital by the time I arrived? They'd been expecting her. They had a bed waiting for her and she was in it within fifteen minutes of our arrival at the hospital. After running around here like a mad woman taking care of Dad and bitching and moaning and making lists of things for me to do for Dad in her absence and showing me where everything was—his

pills and the numbers for the doctor and everything else—
her breathing was stilted and she had these pains in her
chest (I'm sure the chain smoking just helped immensely),
and when she was finally in the hospital bed she looked
more peaceful than I'd ever seen her. Almost happy.

Shortly after I left the hospital Saturday, they sent
Mom into the ICU. It's like she had been sitting here for
months just waiting for me to get out here to see to Dad so
she could go properly over the edge the second I showed up.
Alan, I'm telling you the minute she saw me she was finally
able to stop holding it all back. It was like everything in her
body failed the minute she saw me.

We were there for three hours on Sunday. We went to
see her but they were running tests on her most of the day.
When they wheeled her back into the room and settled her in
bed, I asked her how she felt and she waved her hand at me like
she was fine, never mind. Then she looked over my shoulder to
see if Dad was there, and she said, Where's your father?

I told her he was having a cup of coffee in the
cafeteria and she pointed her finger at me. I thought she
was going to scold me for leaving him alone for two seconds,
but she wanted me to come closer so she could whisper to
me. So I came up close to her bed and she said, Get that
man out of my house.

Her first lucid moment after the ICU and that's
what she said. Get that man out of my house.

I asked her what was going on and she waved her
hand again to erase my question. She tells me there's one
of those inter-office envelopes with the string and the little
wheels to wrap the string around and it was under her bras
in the top right drawer of her dresser and that I should read
everything in it, and to make sure Dad didn't see any of it.
Go, now, she tells me. I don't want to see him.

Anyway, in the envelope at home there's a stack of brochures for nursing homes and on the top of the pile is one for Rosewood Gardens just outside of Burlington with a Post-it attached, and the Post-it says, AUDREY, THIS IS THE ONE! It was underlined three times. Another Post-it had the phone number for the director of admissions at Rosewood and a letter with it explaining that there's usually a long waiting list but it works on a triage-type basis and she had already taken him for testing at the hospital last week and so there's only a ten-day wait for Dad because of how bad he is. I can only imagine what she told them to push his admission through.

Mom has it all set up for him to be admitted on April 8, so it looks like I'm going to be stuck here until at least the ninth, maybe even the tenth. I know that makes things crazy for you with your convention. When I talked to Dex tonight he said Sandy was fine with them hanging there for the weekend and getting them to their baseball games. Dex sounds like he's a grown man. I feel I've been here for years.

And you know, all I could think while I'm going through this whole pile of shit my mother left me was, You bitch. You fucking bitch. You had this all planned. The hospital stay and everything. Could she have done that? Planned a trip to the ICU, like that?

From: Audrey Taylor <ataylor@ameritech.net>
To: Alan Taylor <alantaylor@comcast.net>
Date: Tue, 01 Apr 2008 01:22:45 +0000

Alan,
Hi. I don't think I asked about the boys yesterday. I'm sure they're fine. I forgot to tell you about lunches and everything

for when they're back in school next week. I'm sorry I'm saying anything about this. As if you don't know how to make lunches, but Sammy likes peanut butter spread pretty thin on that soft Italian bread I always used to get right from the shelf at the deli. I don't know if you still make bread on Sundays but they both used to love peanut butter on your bread on Mondays. Dex likes hard salami from the Jewel but only the Volpi brand. Sliced thinly, and only four or five slices. They both like their sandwiches cut into four squares. No mustard or anything. And then just chips and fruit snacks and an apple for both of them, and maybe if you have cookies or something, too. Just ask them. Sorry about this, Alan. It feels like I'm falling short everywhere.

Remember my prediction of hell breaking loose? It broke. It's Dantean. More tomorrow. I'm tired.

From: Audrey Taylor <ataylor@ameritech.net>
To: Alan Taylor <alantaylor@comcast.net>
Date: Tue, 01 Apr 2008 13:30:45 +0000

Alan,

I just read over the update I wrote you last night. I guess it was this morning, actually. All that about the boys' lunches and they're still on spring break. I hope they're having a nice break.

I take back what I said about Mom being a bitch the other day. How she put up with him all these years is a mystery. He and I got into an argument over driving last night. It started on the way to the garage. He kept reaching for the car keys in my hand.

Give me the keys, Audrey, he kept saying. Like I was a child. This is the last time I'm gonna ask you, Audrey. Now give me the keys.

I kept saying, I'll drive, Dad. I don't think you should be driving.

Goddamn it, he said. I'll drive. It's my car, and I'm your father, and I'm going to drive.

We were standing at the trunk of the car and the garage door was open and I kept thinking, Should I let him drive? I could see he was getting angry, but I kept thinking how crazy it would be to hand him the keys and let him drive. I was thinking, What if he got into another accident, and all of a sudden an image of the car half inside that school playground, flashed in front of me and I kept hearing your voice saying things like, What? You actually handed the keys over to him and let him drive the car?

So I kept saying no to him. I tried to walk around him to get to the door and that's when he shoved me against the car. His arm was like a piece of wood across my body and my head hit the roof of the car and I was pinned there. I couldn't even breathe let alone move, and I was crying, and I said, Okay, Dad. Okay. Let me go, now. You can drive. And he said, Give me the keys. I'll let you go when you give me the keys. And that's what I did. I dropped the keys. I actually hoped for a second that we would get in an accident.

And then I got in the passenger side and pulled my seat belt so tight it was hard to breathe, and even after we left the driveway and turned onto Fairview he was still mumbling, I'm driving. I'm driving. I was crying and his knuckles were white on the steering wheel and he kept loosening his fingers and then re-gripping the wheel and he kept saying, I'm driving. I'm driving. It was like it was the only thing he had left.

So now I'm thinking maybe Mom isn't such a bitch after all and maybe it's all taking a toll on her and maybe Dad needs to go to that place.

Tomorrow I'm renting a car. I'm just going to tell him I'm the only one who can drive it. I'm just going to tell him those are the rules. I'll tell him it's policy. He still understands that word.

Dad is taking a nap upstairs. Jesus. My chest hurts and my head is banging.

Also. I forgot to tell you. Yesterday at the hospital, while Mom was sleeping I went to get Dad a sweet roll from the cafeteria, and when I came back to the room the door was closed. I started opening it and he was on the other side seeing to it that I opened the door slowly and without making noise. He had his finger to his lips. Mom is sleeping, he says, like if it weren't for him she'd be awake and everything would be wrong. He thinks he's taking care of her.

He had his chair set up at the door to make sure the nurses were aware that she was sleeping, too. And while he was sitting in the chair reading the paper, Mom turned her head toward me. She wasn't even sleeping. At her side her fingers curled toward her to call me, and she whispered again that she wanted him out of her house. I'm not going home until he's gone, she said.

I know, I know, I told her. Five more days.

Look at my arm, she said.

There were bruises on her arm in the shape of his big fingers.

They're worse on the left arm, she said. And she started to show them to me but the sleeve of her robe was tucked under her butt and her arm was kind of stuck so I was like, That's okay, Mom, I believe you. You don't have to show me.

The night he did this to me, she said, I also stepped in his shit, she said. Middle of the night on my way to the bathroom. After he did this to me. How's that? she said.

Bruises on my arm and his shit between my toes. Did you
ever feel human feces between your toes, Audrey?

My mother puts sentences together that I've never
heard anyone say. Sentences I've never read before.

From: Audrey Taylor <ataylor@ameritech.net>
To: Alan Taylor <alantaylor@comcast.net>
Date: Tue, 01 Apr 2008 23:15:21 +0000

I thought you might have responded to at least one of my
emails by now. I suppose it doesn't matter. Sammy was so
sweet last night when I talked to him. I said good night to
him and before he hung up the phone he said, Don't you
want to talk to Dad?
I lied to him. I said, No, I talked to him earlier, sweetie.

This mess over here is never-ending. I can't believe
I haven't told you this, yet. The fact that I haven't yet
mentioned it, tells you just how crazy it's been.

You wouldn't believe my mornings. Every day. Same
thing. He comes down for coffee and the first thing he does
is he confuses me with Mom.

Where is everybody? he says. I tell him it's just you
and me, Dad.

Where's Audrey? he says.

I'm right here, Dad, I tell him.

Oh, that's right. That's right, he says.

Where's your sister, Mary?

She's in Atlanta, I tell him.

By herself?

No, she's married, Dad. She has two girls and a boy.

My grandchildren, he says.

That's right, Dad.

What are their names? he says.

Allison, Annabelle, and Alex, I tell him.

What about Bob? he says.

I tell him he's still in San Francisco.

What does he do for a living now?

Something in advertising, I tell him.

Is that right? he says.

Yes, Dad.

Good money in that, he says.

I guess so, I say.

And you're a teacher, he says.

Yes, Dad.

Summers off, he says. That's nice. And you're married, too, right?

That's right, Dad, I say.

To Alan?

Yes, Dad.

He's a teacher, too, right?

Not anymore, Dad, I tell him. He's an attorney for the city.

Big shot, huh?

Not really, Dad. He's just an attorney for the Chicago Police. (No offense, Alan.)

And then he asks me for a sheet of paper and a pencil and here's what we do, Alan. We make a list of dead people. That's what we do.

My brother Charlie's dead, he says.

Yes, I say.

And he writes Charlie's name on the list.

He drowned at an altar boy picnic.

Yes, I tell him.

He was twelve, he says.

Yes.

I was thirteen, he says.

Yes.

I wasn't right there when it happened, he says. I was playing softball in the field on the other end of the park.

And I don't say anything. I always worry that it'll make him sad, that it'll be a re-mourning.

There wasn't anything I could do, he says.

I know, Dad, I tell him.

Making the list is never as sad as I think it's going to be. It's just a list we make. Same list every day.

You know, we did this yesterday, I tell him. I have the list from yesterday.

I know, he says. I hate to be a bother, Audrey, he says, but do you mind if we do it again? And then he begins asking questions about people who are still alive.

He asks about you. How are Alan and the boys? he says.

I tell him everyone is fine. This is where I mix it up a bit. Some days I tell him about Dex. I tell him Dex is crazy about baseball, and he asks me what position he plays, and I tell him shortstop and pitcher, and one day I told him that Dex dressed up as Kim Jong Il last Halloween. Then I had to tell him how Kim Jong Il was the North Korean dictator and he asked me how Dex knew who was the North Korean dictator and I told him he must have been watching something on television about him or he must have read it in the newspaper or something. I don't think they teach them about North Korea in school, do they?

However he learned about him, it definitely wasn't from me. I had to Google it just to learn how to spell it to write this email to you. I told him how disappointed Dex was that no one knew who he was trying to be.

Then he said, You should have given him one of them Hello, My Name Is stickers.

Then he said, sometimes I forget names.

I talk more about Sammy, too, and how good he is at hockey and basketball and baseball. I told him Sammy beat you playing basketball in the driveway the other day. I know it happened last summer but I told him it was just the other day, because he doesn't need to know everything. And then he asked if you were mad that Sammy beat you at one-on-one and I told him you didn't get mad. That you hardly ever got mad and you were a pretty good sport about it, but that you looked pretty tired afterward. I told him Sammy went in the house and got you a glass of ice water and said to you, Now I know where I got my hustle from.

Everything he says reminds me that you and I are still separated. He asked if you still trimmed the hedges and I told him yes you did, and then he asked if you still took care of the laundry and I said yes you still did, and he said I think that's great that he does the laundry. He remembers when he slept on the downstairs couch that summer the boys got the bobblehead trophies for Little League and left the trophies on the dryer for months. He used to sit on the couch and watch the heads bounce around to the vibrations of the dryer.

After he said that bit about the bobbleheads he was quiet for a while and then he said, I did the laundry once. And his head was bobbing a little bit and I knew that he was still thinking about the bobbleheads on the dryer. I ruined one of your mother's sweaters, and then she asked me never to do laundry again, so I never did.

I told him that you had a couple shirts that couldn't be dried so you knew a little something about that, and I said there were also some things I didn't put in the hamper because they needed special care. I told him I put those things on top of the dryer and that you didn't do anything with those clothes. I told him you just leave them there for me and I do a special load of laundry once a week or so.

After I told him that he asked me why I was crying. I told him I wasn't sure.

He thought that was a pretty good idea about the special clothes being put to the side. He said I should get a little hamper, just a little one. Something small enough to put on top of the dryer for my special clothes. I could even put your shirts in it, he said. The ones that shouldn't go in the dryer.

Every morning he asks if the bobbleheads are still on the dryer. Every morning.

Some mornings I feel like I should just tell him everything. It's not like he would remember. The things you want him to forget he remembers, the things you want him to remember he forgets.

From: Audrey Taylor <ataylor@ameritech.net>
To: Alan Taylor <alantaylor@comcast.net>
Date: Wed, 02 Apr 2008 23:43:02 +0000

Alan,

You probably saw my parents' phone number come up on your BlackBerry screen last night. I hung up before you could answer. I feel like Mom and Dad are sucking the life out of me. I'm literally drained. At first I was pissed that you couldn't take two minutes to respond to a single email, but now I realize I don't want you to. Right now I need you to do exactly what you're doing. Be there for the boys.

I was going through Dad's things this afternoon looking for the title to his car and I found an old journal of yours. I guess I must have taken it from your desk when I came here for that week after Isabel. I don't know why I would have taken it with me here.

I spent all day wondering if I should read it. It felt like a betrayal, but I finally started to read it. I don't remember ever reading it before last night. I don't even remember the events. It's such a fog, Alan. Those days.

I'm sure you're sleeping already, but promise me tomorrow you'll kiss the boys good night for me. Tell Sammy this for me before he falls asleep: Sweet dreams, good night, I love you.

And finger-comb Dex's hair for me and tell him I said, Dream away, my love. Tell him I said that.

There's so much more, Alan, but I'm really tired. And tomorrow I will have to get up early to review the dead.

From: Audrey Taylor <ataylor@ameritech.net>
To: Alan Taylor <alantaylor@comcast.net>
Date: Thur, 03 Apr 2008 13:02:02 +0000

Hi.

This morning after we made the list I took Dad to the grocery store in the rental car. He seemed to understand why he couldn't drive the car, though he wondered why I needed to rent a car at all. He said it was an unnecessary expense and that I was just like my mother when it came to those things. I told him you were thinking of buying a new car and you thought this was a great way to consider the car. That it was like a test drive. He told me he thought you were a prudent fellow. That's what he said. But right after that, he said, He's thinking of buying a Taurus? There were italics on the word when he asked that.

He still makes me laugh sometimes.

From: Audrey Taylor <ataylor@ameritech.net>
To: Alan Taylor <alantaylor@comcast.net>
Date: Thur, 03 Apr 2008 19:34:02 +0000

Alan,

I read this journal of yours and it seems as though you think Isabel was only your daughter. That she wasn't mine as well. This is what you wrote in your journal on June 23, 2004, almost two years after Isabel died:

It's been three days since Audrey has said a word to any of us. When we bumped into each other near the refrigerator I almost reminded her that she still has two sons. I had it all planned. I was going to say, Excuse me, Audrey, I know that Isabel is gone, but I just want to remind you that you still have two sons. The oldest is named Dex. He's ten. And the youngest is Sammy. He's six. Six years old. Two sons. Audrey is their mother. This is my wife. Three fucking days.

I was in a bad place, Alan. I don't know what else to say.

I don't know why I'm even reading this thing. I'm sorry.

From: Audrey Taylor <ataylor@ameritech.net>
To: Alan Taylor <alantaylor@comcast.net>
Date: Thur, 03 Apr 2008 23:50:27 +0000

Hi, Alan.

More updates from the madhouse. While we were making our list of the dead this morning, and we came to the part where he brings up his parents, Dad said, My mother is dead, and I said, Yes. And then he said, My father died two days later, and I said, Yes, Dad, and then he was quiet for a while.

Did we make this list yesterday? he said.

Yes, Dad, I said.

Is it okay if we do it again?

Yes, Dad. It's okay, I told him.

Today he said he wanted to see their graves, but I told him they were buried in a cemetery in Milwaukee, Wisconsin.

No, I'm pretty sure they're buried here in Iowa, he said. I know where the cemetery is.

And so I didn't argue with him. The guy at Rosewood said I shouldn't argue with Dad when he insists something is this way or that way when it's really not. He said it just aggravates them more. So Dad said, Why don't you drive me there? And I didn't say anything.

Did I ask you to drive me there yesterday?

No, Dad.

Good, he said.

You can drive that car you rented, he said, and I figured it was better than staying here and reading your journal all afternoon and so we took a forty-five-minute drive, him looking out the window and tapping his fingernail against the glass like the place was supposed to be right around the corner and he just couldn't seem to figure out the street, and then finally he said, I think maybe you're right about them being in Milwaukee. That's where they used to live, he said.

He seemed aware that we had spent time doing this, and he apologized for taking up my time. Then he went quiet.

From: Audrey Taylor <ataylor@ameritech.net>
To: Alan Taylor <alantaylor@comcast.net>
Date: Fri, 04 Apr 2008 01:25:07 +0000

Alan,

Do you remember the day I surprised you at the Newberry Library? Isabel was maybe eighteen months old or something and I walked in there with Isabel on my arm and said, Let's go, nerd. We're going to the beach. Do you remember that day? I had a cooler packed with sandwiches and olives and chips from Alpine Deli and we went to North Avenue Beach. You had a ponytail then. Isabel had that green floppy beach hat on and she was naked the whole day and we took a million photographs of her. We were happy that day weren't we, Alan? And on the way home, while Isabel slept in the baby seat do you remember what I did? I took my top off and leaned back on the passenger side and you touched my breasts all the way home. Do you remember making love to me when we came home that afternoon? Do you remember that day, Alan? Maybe you wrote about that story in one of your old journals.

From: Audrey Taylor <ataylor@ameritech.net>
To: Alan Taylor <alantaylor@comcast.net>
Date: Fri, 04 Apr 2008 13:31:21 +0000

Hi, Alan.

We went to see Mom at the hospital this morning and Dad asked her what all the wires were for. She said she needed them, and he said, No, you don't need them. You just need to come home.

They're taking care of me here, she told him.

You need to come home, he said again and he started getting angrier. I'll take care of you at home, he said.

I was afraid he was going to pull all the wires right out of her skin, and I was afraid to stop him because of when he pushed me up against his car the other night, and so I rang the button for the nurse. And the nurse came and she said, You need to take your father out of here, and so I told him we had tickets to see a movie, and before I left I kissed Mom good-bye and she said, Audrey, I can't live with him anymore, and I knew she was right.

And I said, I know, Mom. I know. Two more days.

Do you promise? she said, and I said, Yes, I promise.

We didn't have tickets, of course, because I hadn't planned on him going crazy at the hospital. I didn't even know what movies were playing or what time they were playing or anything, so we just drove to the theater downtown and bought two tickets for the next movie that was playing, which was the cartoon of *The King and I.*

He was fine for maybe five minutes and then he turned to me and said, Where's Audrey? And I said, Right here, Dad. I'm right here.

Oh, that's right, he said. And then five more minutes passed and he asked again. Same thing. Where's Audrey?

He started to get agitated and more and more upset, because he knew that he'd asked me a number of times where I was. He started sweating.

I know she's somewhere out there, he said. This is bad, he said. This is bad. She's supposed to be with us.

Dad. I'm right here, I said again. I've grown up. I'm here now.

No, you're not, he said. Audrey's a little girl. Look, he said. I hate to be a bother about this, but we've got to do something.

People in the theater started shushing us. So we left. We got in the car, and he started sweating like crazy and talking fast while he was looking out the window for me. Turning his head and looking through every window.

We drove around for more than an hour, Alan, and the whole time we were out there we were looking for me.

You take your eyes off them for a minute, he said, and they go for miles. Every time you turn around. There's no end to the worrying.

This is bad, he kept saying.

I swear to god I thought this, Alan: There will be no end to this night. This night will never end. We will forever be driving in this car looking for me.

She's so little, he kept saying. She's so little.

You know what? I finally said. I just remembered she's at a friend's house. She's at her friend's house. She's okay.

We have to get home, then, he said, because she'll be home, soon.

And I figured that was better than driving all around the city, so I took him home.

I was exhausted. We parked the car and I was at the top of the stairs and looked back at him and he was sweating. He was pale as a ghost.

I don't know who he thought I was but I asked him if he wanted me to call Mom, and he said, Yes, that's what he thought I should do.

So I just dialed her number at the hospital and handed the phone to him and as he asked her, Where's Audrey? I realized that Mom didn't know any of this was going on, and I could hear her voice in the receiver saying, She's supposed to be with you, Jerry. And I just took the phone from him and I said, Mom, I'm right here. Dad doesn't know who I am. Just tell him I'm Audrey and that I'm not a little girl anymore. I don't care if he gets aggravated. I can't do this anymore.

And then Mom spoke to him and he was fine. He went to his room. I thought he would fall asleep immediately, but he came downstairs ten minutes later as I was pouring myself a glass of wine. I heard him coming up behind me but I didn't turn around. He asked where his car was, and I told him it was in the garage. He asked if I was sure, and I said I was sure, and he asked if he could go out there to see it, and I slammed the bottle of wine down and said, No, Dad. You can't, okay? Your goddamn car is in the garage and I'm tired. So just go back upstairs and go to bed.

And then I didn't hear anything behind me. I sipped from my glass of wine and set it down and then turned around and he was just standing there like a little child on the verge of tears.

May I just hold the keys? he said.

He was like a little boy standing there, Alan.

I'll just take the keys to my room and I won't go to the garage, he said.

So I gave him the keys and he looked at me so sweetly. Like a little boy.

Thanks, he said, and he went to his room.

From: Audrey Taylor <ataylor@ameritech.net>
To: Alan Taylor <alantaylor@comcast.net>
Date: Sat, 05 Apr 2008 13:25:53 +0000

Hey.

Tomorrow I take Dad to Rosewood. Mom comes home from the hospital the next day. It's like she planned it perfectly. I haven't even told Dad about Rosewood yet. The guy there said not to say anything to him about it until the day we admit him. It feels like there's a lump in my chest like a balloon. It goes away for a little while and then it feels like it's inflating again.

I'll probably stay with Mom on Monday and through Tuesday and come home on Wednesday. I mean I'll come back. I'll come back on Wednesday to pick up the boys.

I know you're in San Francisco now, so I don't suppose I'll hear from you until we're both back in the city. I looked over your journal again. That entry about Isabel. It was odd to see her name in your handwriting, Alan. I think that's what the balloon under my ribcage is from. I haven't heard you say her name in years.

I wasn't being perfectly honest when I told you about our morning routine over here. When Dad begins his list of the dead each morning he doesn't write his brother Charlie's name down like I said he does. The first name he writes on the list is Isabel's.

And after he writes Isabel's name on the list of the dead, he looks up and says, Isabel is dead.

When he says that, it's the saddest he ever gets. Isabel is dead, he says. He looks me in the eye and it's like he's all there again. He mentions the newspaper articles and the search and when they finally found her body. He says that Mom clipped the articles and saved them. They're somewhere around here, he tells me. I keep forgetting to ask her about them, he says.

And after that is when he writes down Charlie's name.

My brother Charlie is dead, too, he says.

Yes, I say.

He drowned at an altar boy picnic, he says.

Yes, I tell him.

Charlie was twelve when he died, he says.

Yes, I say.

Same as Isabel, he says. Same age as when they found Isabel's body.

Five years go by without either of us—you or me—ever saying Isabel's name, and I come here where my father sits at the table and disappears before me a little bit more each day and I listen to him say Isabel's name a half dozen times every morning.

Same age as when they found Isabel, he says.

I was thirteen at the picnic, he says.

Yes.

I wasn't there when it happened, he says. I was playing softball in the field when it happened.

Were you there? he says. Were you there when it happened to Isabel?

Every day I tell him no. I wasn't there, I tell him.

Was Alan there? he asks.

No, I tell him. Neither one of us was there.

Every day except for today. And I don't know if I told him the truth because it was going to be his last day in this house, or if it was because I knew if I told him a week ago, I'd have to tell him the same thing for another seven days straight. I might have told him the answer because I'd been thinking about it every day because he asked me about it every day, and because I'd been reading your journal all week. I'm not sure why I finally told him, Alan. But I told him.

I told him that that was a tough question to answer. In a way, I said, Alan and I were both there when it happened, and in a way we weren't there.

I told him that Isabel and Sammy and I picked you up from O'Hare after the Madagascar trip and how we went to Khyber Pass. I told him Dex wasn't there because he was at Jack Murphy's house for the all-star team sleepover. I told him the story we related to you about the kids getting lost at the arts festival in Evanston. I told him how you were crying in the restaurant, and I told him about how Izzy was acting like Daisy Buchanan all night.

I even told him that as soon as Isabel and Sammy were in bed for the night, we had amazing welcome home sex. What do I care, he'll forget about it by tomorrow.

Then what? he said.

Then we started arguing, I said.

I told him we got into it pretty good. About the kids missing out on you every summer you went on these research trips, about how difficult it was taking care of three kids all by myself, about how they were growing up without a father. Then I told him it somehow all came around to an argument about Isabel. How she was growing up and acting like Daisy Buchanan all of a sudden, and how she had to flirt with you to get your attention and you didn't even seem to notice she was flirting with you. The whole summer long I'd been watching her turn into a woman all of a sudden. But something wasn't right about it, Alan. I kept thinking she was turning into what she thought it meant to be a woman. And all summer long I was thinking that the model she had of women was me, and at the same time she was becoming a woman with interests in men, she was living with a woman whose husband was making a choice to leave his wife. And I kept thinking her belief system of men and women was being built on how to keep a man from leaving her, and that somehow that had to do with being sexy. You kept a man around by being sexy. And I was pissed, Alan. I was pissed that on top of being a mother to two boys and a mother to a girl, and on top of having to serve as a model for womanhood, I also had to make excuses for my own womanhood.

And I told him how we went to bed pissed at each other, too. How we went to bed thinking that Isabel and Sammy were sound asleep in their bedrooms, not having any idea that it was probably our fighting that drove Isabel out of the house.

Then my Dad said, But you weren't there, really. You weren't really there when it happened exactly.

No, Dad, I wasn't right there with her when it happened, I said. But I wish I had been.

But if I had been there, Alan, I probably wouldn't be here at Rosewood writing you these updates from Iowa. I'd probably be dead, too. That would be something to write in your journal.

Isabel was my daughter, too, Alan.

From: Audrey Taylor <ataylor@ameritech.net>
To: Alan Taylor <alantaylor@comcast.net>
Date: Sun, 06 Apr 2008 23:50:39 +0000

Hi.

I took Dad to Rosewood this afternoon. After we made the list of the dead this morning I told him I was going to take him to the nursing home for a couple of days. That's what the guy at Rosewood said to say.

Does your mother know this? he said.

Yes, I said.

Are you certain? he said.

Yes, I said.

Can we go to the hospital and see what Mom has to say about this? he said.

Yes.

At the hospital he asked Mom if it was true.

Yes, she said.

Why? he said.

Jerry, you need to do this for us, she said. For me.

And he said okay. Just like that.

I can't take care of you anymore, she said.

And he said okay again.

Just until I get better, she said.

That's what the guy at Rosewood told her to say.

I'll have to pack a suitcase, he said.

I already have your things in the car, I said, and he looked at me like he'd just learned I had played a trick on him.

I can see that you're ready for me to go, he said. And for a minute it seemed like there was nothing wrong with him.

I figured I'd stay with him until he went to sleep in his room. At first he didn't want to put his pajamas on. He kept saying, No, thank you, Audrey, I'm fine just like this.

And so he was lying there in his pants and his shirt and after a while he got up and said, I think I'll put my pajamas on now, and he went in the bathroom and changed.

I was sitting on the chair next to his bed when he came out with his pajamas on. He had his pants and his shirt folded in his hands and he set them on the shelf there and he got into bed.

He turned on his side and looked at me for a while and then he patted the bed next to him and I sat there, combing his hair with my fingers, and then I lay down next to him and brushed my fingers across his forehead.

You're a good girl, he said. I love you. He kept saying that. You're a good girl, Audrey. You're a good girl.

I'll call you tomorrow. I couldn't even tell you what day it is today without putting serious thought into it.

I'd like to see you when I get home, Alan. With the boys. I'm not sure if I can handle another day without seeing you all in one place. I'd actually like to talk.

CHAPTER 9

The Baseball Guy
(April 17, 2008)

Mom was only home from Iowa for four days when Grandma's neighbor called our house and told us Grandma died. Sammy and I had to take off a few days of school to go to Iowa to bury her and to sell the house and also to visit Grandpa at the old folks' home where he stays. What was weird about the whole thing was that we all took the trip together: Mom, Dad, Sammy, and me. We were all there in Dad's car. It wasn't that weird that we were all in the same car together—sometimes that happens. But this wasn't just a short ride to the skating rink or to a restaurant or a baseball game, this was a long ride to another state, and we also got out of a few days of school to do it, and so it was more like a vacation. I remember looking at Sammy in the backseat next to me just to see if he felt how weird it was, too, but he was like, *Why are you staring at me, Dex?*

All the way there Mom leaned up against the door on the passenger side, looking out the window like she was trying to find something. A couple of times I scooted up on the hump between the seats to talk to Dad because I thought it must have felt weird for him to be in the car with all of us and no one to talk to, but Mom would just start crying all of a sudden while we were talking, or she would say, "Dex, sweetie, better sit back and buckle up."

The first thing we did was go visit Grandpa. Mom went in to talk to him first. She said she wanted to tell him herself that Grandma died. After about fifteen minutes she came back out and told us that she told him. Dad asked how he was, and Mom shrugged and said he seemed fine, but maybe that we shouldn't say anything about Grandma to him when we went in there.

When we went in, though, right away Grandpa asked why Grandma wasn't with us and I was afraid Sammy was going to slip and say that she died, but Mom gave us both a look and shook her head. I was thinking, *Don't look at me, Sammy's the one you should be worrying about.* But Sammy didn't say anything either. He didn't even look at Grandpa. He was looking around the room, sort of as though he was smelling it.

Mom just told Grandpa that Grandma wasn't feeling well.

That first night, Sammy and I stayed up pretty late watching ESPN Sports Center and a delayed-broadcast baseball game. After breakfast the next morning, when Mom and Dad went to the funeral home to make the arrangements, we watched *The Sandlot* DVD, which was the only movie we brought with us that Sammy felt like watching. I didn't care what movie we put in because I knew I wasn't going to watch it. I also knew that Sammy was going to fall asleep after a little while of watching the movie, because he was already drowsy at breakfast because of how late we stayed up. Plus, he can fall asleep anywhere.

So we watched *The Sandlot* for a while and when Sammy fell asleep on the couch, I went to Grandma's desk where she used to sit when she wrote checks to pay the bills. She used to call it *the homework center* when we came to visit. Even if it was the summertime she would make us do homework there. She had math and vocabulary workbooks for us, and a stack of crossword puzzles, too.

I opened the top drawer of the desk that was always unlocked and where the paper clips and rubber bands were, and the key was still there where it always was. But before I did anything I checked again to see if Sammy was really sleeping or if he was just faking. He was breathing slow and deep, though, and so I knew he was really sleeping. Before I went back to the homework center I checked the door to make sure it was locked so that at least I would hear Mom or Dad jiggling the keys in the door which would give me enough time to throw everything back in the big bottom drawer of the desk and close it and then run back into the TV room and make like I had always been there. When I sat at the desk again and opened my hand there was an impression of the key on my palm, I was holding it so tight.

Everything was still there in a big envelope in the bottom drawer. All the articles from the *Chicago Sun-Times* and the *Chicago Tribune* that Grandma had cut out of the newspapers. All the articles had the same photograph of Isabel. It was the only photograph of her I ever saw. At home there were no baby pictures or birthday pictures or any other pictures of her. The only time I ever got to see her photo was at Grandma's house and this was the photo, the newspaper photo of her from probably the sixth grade. She was twelve the summer she died.

I didn't read all the articles because I wasn't sure how long Mom and Dad were going to be at the funeral home. I flipped through them to find the one with the date of August 24, written out in Grandma's handwriting in blue pen at the top. It was the earliest date of any of the articles. It was two days after Dad came home from the trip to Madagascar, where he was studying ring-tailed lemurs for the summer. Even though I know he knows a lot about animals it's still hard to imagine him as a scientist. After Isabel died he became obsessed with studying law and became a lawyer for the city.

I read the August 24 article again. It was the one that said what everyone was doing that last night that anybody saw Isabel, which was eating at a restaurant called Khyber Pass. It explained what I was doing that night, too, which was playing in an all-star game for kid-pitch baseball. The article didn't have all the information about the game, but I remember everything. We were playing the River Forest All-Stars, and we lost by a score of 9–8 even though we were winning 5–1 after four innings. We were winning until Coach Roy took out his son because his son mouthed off when Coach Roy told him to quit pouting. And then Robbie Malloy came in to pitch and he got rocked by the River Forest All-Stars and we lost 9–8. They had five lefties on that team and all of them were bigger than anyone on our team. I also remember that the River Forest All-Stars all had official baseball bags hooked up against the dugout fence. And they had two sets of jerseys, one set for home games and one set for away games.

After the game I had a sleepover at Jack Murphy's house, which was also mentioned in the article. I don't even think Jack Murphy knows his name was in the newspaper. I know I never told him about it because the article wasn't about something you would put on a refrigerator.

So I read it three times while Sammy was sleeping in front of the TV, but there was nothing else in the article about that night that would make me remember something more about Isabel. I didn't really think there would be. Not if I hadn't found anything in the article all the other times I had read it. I guess I was thinking that maybe since I was older I might find something in the article I had missed all those other times.

I didn't read the rest of the articles. I only read them once a couple of years ago when I was eleven, and I wished I didn't even read them that one time. I didn't read the article with the date of September 9 at the top in Grandma's handwriting—the one about when they found Isabel's bra in the forest. It had a broken clasp, and the article said it was very muddy. I didn't read the article on September 10, either, which is when they found the book she had with her. It was *The Great Gatsby*. I have read it four times since then. Or the day of October 8, when they found Isabel's body floating in the river naked. But I might as well have read them again because I still remember everything that was in the articles. All I needed to do was see the date at the top of the articles in Grandma's handwriting. In fact when those dates come by every year—September 9, September 10, and October 8—all I think about are the articles with those dates at the top of them and automatically I remember all the things that the articles were writing about. So I might as well have read them again. Maybe, like I said, since I was older I would have found something in them that would have given me something good to remember about Isabel.

I put all of the articles back in the brown envelope except for the one from August 24, which was about the night she disappeared. And what I did with that article is I folded it just so that I could see the photograph of Isabel but nothing else, none of the words of the article. And then I started to think about something I couldn't ever remember thinking before and that was how that night at Khyber Pass was wasted on my parents and my brother, Sammy.

I heard a sound right about then and so I checked the front door to see if it was still locked. I rattled the knob of the door twice which reminded me of the mean guy who lives across the alley from Dad's house. After he locks his door he rattles the doorknob and then stops and then rattles it again and then stops and he does that again and again. His record for a while was fifty-eight times and then this summer he did it eighty-five times. Sammy and I call him Frollo, which is Sammy's nickname for him. He gave it to him after we watched the video of *The Hunchback of Notre Dame*, which has a villain in it named Frollo.

While I was checking to see if the door was locked I also checked on Sammy again to see if he was still sleeping, which he was, and I realized that I was saying this out loud: *Wasted. Wasted. Wasted.*

All the time I was checking the door and checking on Sammy, I was saying *wasted, wasted, wasted*, because the night at Khyber Pass was wasted on all of them—on Mom and Dad and on my brother, Sammy. I was only eight back then and I wasn't even there with them because of the all-star game. I wasn't even there on the last night they saw Isabel. I know for a fact though that it would not have been wasted on me if I had been there.

All the time I was growing up with Sammy he was always saying how I was so lucky because kids who were eight years old got to do so much more than four-year-olds got to do. Kids who were eight got to play baseball and not just stupid tee ball, and kids who were eight got to play in all-star tournaments after the regular season if they were good enough to be on the all-star team. And he used to say always how it was unfair because sometimes four-year-olds were better at baseball than some eight-year-olds, which was true in Sammy's case. In fact all of those things he thought about older kids were true, but what Sammy had no idea about was how in this case he was the lucky one because four-year-olds don't remember anything.

If you were eight when something bad happened you remembered everything. But being four was better than being a grown-up. If you were the father or the mother and a bad thing happened, you probably remembered everything, too. You remembered it but you did whatever you had to do to make yourself forget. Like for example you would put all the photographs of Isabel away somewhere and never talk about her.

Being eight years old in this case was worse than being any age. If you were eight years old and something bad happened you remembered everything. You didn't even have to be in the same place as the bad thing that happened because you have an imagination. You imagine that you were there during whatever the bad experience or thing was. If a bra is found, for example, and the clasp is broken, and it is muddied up, you imagine *how* the clasp was broken and *how* the bra was taken off and *how* it got so dirty. And if a book is found you think of the person who lost the book, or the person who the book was *taken* from, and you imagine how she felt about the book. You wonder what made her carry a book around in the summertime, and you think she must have liked the book a lot if she was carrying it around in the summertime when she was not even being forced to read, and you imagine how she must have felt to have the book taken from her.

It is especially bad to think about the book if you remember that summer how Isabel used to force you and Sammy to attend the Lunch Theater events she put on in her bedroom, where she bribed you with grilled cheese and pickles and potato chips and tomato soup and soda and forced you to watch her act out scenes from *The Great Gatsby* with costumes and everything.

Sometimes it makes you wish, like when you're walking through the park on your way to a baseball game or when you're walking home from school, that you could just see someone doing something bad to another person. It makes you imagine all the ways you would kill a bad guy.

It is possible that it's worse *not* knowing exactly what happened because maybe you imagine something worse than what actually happened. But then you think no, it's not possible to think of anything worse than what happened, and so that's what you try to do: you try to think of something even worse. And then you realize there is always some worse thing to imagine.

It is possible that being eight years old when something bad happens is the worst age to be, because you remember so much.

Isabel would say to me now, if she heard me saying I wished I were at Khyber Pass that night, she would say, *You don't even like the food at Khyber Pass, Dex.* Which is true, but I could have eaten an entire basket of pita bread at least. But food is not the reason I wish I could have been at Khyber Pass that day. The reason I should have been there at Khyber Pass that night is to see Isabel one last time. The reason I should have been there at Khyber Pass is to see Isabel in her blue shorts and her yellow tank top, which are the clothes she was wearing on that night, according to the article. That's why I should have been there that night, so that I could remember her better. To have that last night to remember her.

When I came home the next day from my overnight at Jack Murphy's house, I didn't ever get out of the Murphys' minivan. Mom came to the window and said something to Mrs. Murphy, and then Mom and Dad both came to the side of the van and slid open the door to kiss me and hug me, and Mom's face was red. She was definitely crying just before I saw her and I could tell from just looking at her that pretty soon she would be crying again. And then we went straight back to the Murphys' house, which was fine with me then, but now that I'm older I wish I could have stayed at home. If I had stayed home I would have asked my brother, Sammy, what happened that night.

I ended up staying at Jack Murphy's house for a couple more days. Another thing I remember about when I stayed there was that Mrs. Murphy came into the bathroom once when I was sitting on the toilet. For some reason we always had door problems at home. It takes a million tries to lock the front door of our apartment in Chicago in the summertime, for example. And the bathroom doors never have locks on them. Everyone knows at our house that if the bathroom door looks pretty much like it's closed, then someone is in the bathroom—maybe not on the toilet, but someone is doing something in the bathroom. At the Murphys' house, though, if the bathroom door is closed, it doesn't mean anything. And so while I was sitting on the toilet, Mrs. Murphy came in.

I had the box of Band-Aids on the counter to my left, and I had the wrappers from the Band-Aids on the counter and on the floor and on the sink, and I had a Band-Aid on every one of my fingers and on my knees and elbows and I was putting on another one when she came in, so even though she might not have laughed if she caught me on the toilet bowl, she laughed when she saw me on the toilet bowl with Band-Aids everywhere, which is another example of how I remember everything.

When I finally came back home a couple of days later the police were in front of the house and Mrs. Murphy said, "Oh, shit," and she didn't stop the minivan. We drove right back to her house and ate dinner and finally we came back later on and the police were gone.

At bedtime I think, is the first time I asked about Isabel. It was the first time I realized I hadn't seen her for a while. I asked Dad where she was and he said she wasn't home, which I realize now is just like us not saying anything to Grandpa about Grandma dying. I don't remember what Dad actually said, but I knew the police were there earlier, and I definitely knew something was going on, and that something had happened to Isabel, so when I came back and went into my room—which was also Sammy's room—to go to sleep for the night, I heard my parents' voices in the other room.

Then I heard the door close and didn't hear Mom's voice anymore. All I heard was the sound of my father crying. I had never heard that before. I closed the door of our bedroom because I didn't want Dad to know that I knew he was crying. I remember standing there with my hand on the doorknob, which was made of glass—I used to think it was a giant diamond. I was thinking of going out there to check on Dad, but I didn't.

Instead, I woke up Sammy, and he said, "Is it tomorrow already?"

I said no, that it was still today, but that I had to wake him up so I could ask him something. And I asked him what happened that night they picked up Dad from the airport with Isabel. And even though only a few days had passed since then, Sammy said he didn't remember what happened that night.

"But you were there, Sammy," I told him. "How could you not know what happened?"

And he said he didn't know, and again I said, "But you were there the whole time, Sammy. Do you know what restaurant I'm talking about?"

And he said he knew what restaurant I was talking about.

"There's crayons on the table there," I said to him, thinking that this would help him remember the night, and he said, "I know there are crayons because I was drawing Baseball Guy on the tablecloth."

I am the one who showed Sammy how to draw Baseball Guy. It's all he ever used to draw. Baseball Guy is always diving for a baseball with his cap flying off. I had shown Sammy the trick of drawing curved lines to make it look like Baseball Guy was really diving and to make it look like his cap was just then flying off his head.

Sometimes I ask Sammy, now that he's nine years old, if he remembers Baseball Guy, and he immediately smiles and says, "I loved drawing Baseball Guy."

And so Sammy said he remembered that night at the restaurant because he was drawing Baseball Guy while Dad was talking about the jungle, and then he also said that Dad was crying in the restaurant, too. And I said, "Are you sure he was crying in the restaurant?" and he said yes, that he was sure, but he must have been thinking about another day, because if Isabel was there at the restaurant with them, then Isabel wasn't dead yet and there was no reason for my father to cry. And Sammy also said that Dad was telling him about a special tree in the jungle that helped people *stay found*, that's how he said it. I remember him saying it like that, a tree that helped people *stay found*. And I asked him what Isabel was doing, and he said that she was talking to Dad and Mom, and that she was acting out something from her book. That's all she was doing and that's all he remembered.

After that day I started to do everything around the house. I remember Mom couldn't do anything. I was making sandwiches for Sammy, and I was making toast for him for breakfast and buttering it and sprinkling it with cinnamon and sugar, and I was also making toast for Dad before he went to work. I was making sure that our clothes were ready for the next day and that Sammy's clothes matched. And I washed clothes in the washing machine and dried them in the dryer and I would iron them, too, sometimes.

And if there wasn't any lunch meat I made Philadelphia Cream Cheese sandwiches on bread with jelly.

Not long after that is when Dad left his job as a scientist and started going to law school. And about two years later he moved out. First to an apartment not far from us and then to an apartment in Forest Park.

Sometimes we stayed at Dad's house and sometimes we stayed at home. They were still friends, my parents. They were not divorced.

When I heard the keys in the door, I locked the big drawer of the desk in the homework center and put the key in the top drawer, but I didn't put the brown envelope back in the drawer where it was when I found it. Instead of doing that I ran to where my suitcase was in the guest room, and I put the envelope at the bottom of my suitcase under everything else. Then I shoved the suitcase under the bed and went into the kitchen and opened the door of the refrigerator and pretended that that was where I was when Mom and Dad came back home after getting Grandma ready for the funeral.

Dad said, "Hey, kiddo," and I noticed that he was holding Mom's hand. Mom had a white box in her other hand. Then Mom said, "Hi, Dex," and kissed my forehead. I asked her what was in the box and she looked at Dad and said, "A dress."

And she smiled. "There is a dress in the box," she said again. Then she asked where Sammy was, and I said that he fell asleep while we were watching *The Sandlot*, which was true.

I looked at Mom's hand again. It was still in Dad's. They were still holding hands in the kitchen. I went back into the TV room then, and sat on the floor with my back against the couch and my heart still beating fast.

I watched The *Sandlot* for a while and then I remembered about the articles of Isabel. I was thinking then that there was nothing in the articles that was new. And now that I was thirteen I wasn't going to ask my parents anything about Isabel anymore. And just when I was old enough to figure out that Grandma was the only one who might have wanted to talk about Isabel, she was dead, too.

There was also no way I was going to say anything to Sammy about Isabel anymore, because the thing about Sammy is that as soon as he knows someone else is sad, that's it for Sammy. Immediately he is going to be sadder than whoever it was that was already sad.

The most I could do to make it seem like I was talking about Isabel was to ask Sammy every once in a while if he remembered Baseball Guy. It immediately makes him happy whenever I ask him. When I ask him about Baseball Guy, he smiles as if drawing that guy was the best thing about being a little kid and he says he loved Baseball Guy, and always then, to me, it seems like we are not talking about Baseball Guy at all, but that we're talking about Isabel.

On the TV then, came the scene in *The Sandlot* when they are playing night baseball on July Fourth and the only reason they are able to play at night is because of all the lights from the fireworks. In that scene Ray Charles is singing "O beautiful for spacious skies," and I was glad Sammy was still sleeping because he always looks like he's about to cry when that song comes on. Especially during this movie because it is about baseball and there are fireworks and the boys are playing in slow motion and Ray Charles is singing Sammy's favorite song. I start to cry a little, too, when I see it. But still, I couldn't wait for Sammy to wake up pretty soon so I could ask him if he remembered Baseball Guy.

After that scene was over and the song was over I went back to the homework center to get a stack of blank paper and colored pencils. I clipped the paper to a clipboard that Grandma kept on the desk, and I brought it back to where I was sitting against the couch in the TV room and I began to draw Baseball Guy. While I was drawing him I was smiling and thinking of when Sammy would wake up and see what I was drawing.

Dad came into the TV room then, and sat next to me on the couch.

"Where's Mom?" I said, and Dad said she was taking a nap in the guest room, and we were quiet for a little while.

Then Dad whispered to me so that he wouldn't wake up Sammy. He whispered, "What are you drawing?"

"You'll see," I told him, and he was smiling while he waited and so was I. And while I kept drawing Baseball Guy I was thinking about how when Dad walked in the door he was holding Mom's hand, and I kept looking up at him to see if he recognized what I was drawing yet. And then all of a sudden, when I drew the cap and the lines that made it seem his cap was flying off just then because of the pure hustle of his defense, Dad smiled and leaned toward me and said, "Baseball Guy," and I just started to cry. I couldn't help it. I started to cry like a baby, and Dad got down on the floor and put his arm around me. I couldn't stop crying.

"What's wrong, Dex?" he said. "What's wrong?" he said, but nothing was wrong. For some reason I was just so happy he remembered Baseball Guy.

ACKNOWLEDGMENTS

This would never have been a book without Lydia Hankins. And it would have been much less of a book without Gigi Hudson and Michael Pereira. Thank you.

For his continuing and overwhelming encouragement I thank my cousin, Jeff Lombardo.

I thank Adam Davis, Eric Davis, Veronica Vela, Ruth Hutton, Jeff Windus, and Beth Keegan for being my first readers, and Amy Rita for giving space to some of these stories in the Forest Park Post.

I thank Tony Fitzpatrick for his friendship and for the White Rose of Chicago.

Thanks to Gina Frangello, Stacy Bierlein, Allison Parker and Kathryn Kosmeja of OV Books, and the folks at Dzanc Books.

Thanks to my Chicago tribe: Betsy Crane, Megan Stielstra, J. Adams Oaks, and Emily Tedrowe.

And thanks as well to my tribe at Warren Wilson College, and a few of the elders: T.M. McNally, Murad Kalam, Wilton Barnhardt, Charles D'Ambrosio, C.J. Hribal, David Haynes, and Adria Bernardi.

Thanks to Tony Serritella, Daniel Ferri, and Mike Baron, whom I should have thanked in 2005 when "The Logic of a Rose: Chicago Stories" was published.

To my friend, Stephanie Clifford-Martin, and to Anne Calcagno and Fred Shafer, my first teachers.

And to Marc Smith, whose stage at the Green Mill's Uptown Poetry Slam is pretty much to blame for all of this.